BABY BOY BLUE

In 1944, young Walter Buehl finds his mother stabbed to death on the kitchen floor and his teenage brother Tony crouching beside her, bloody knife in hand. Forty-one years later, Tony escapes from a psychiatric hospital, and a series of murders ensues — with Tony as the main suspect. But Lieutenant Asher Lowenstein isn't convinced of Tony's guilt, and he asks his friend, psychic Tam Westington, to help. As the police conduct a manhunt for the Baby Boy Blue killer, a long-buried truth may surface — at the cost of more lives. . .

MARILYN BRAHEN

BABY BOY BLUE

Complete and Unabridged

LINFORD
Leicester

First published in Great Britain

First Linford Edition
published 2014

A catalogue record for this book is available
from the British Library.

ISBN 978–1–4448–2084–3

Published by
F. A. Thorpe (Publishing)
Anstey, Leicestershire

Set by Words & Graphics Ltd.
Anstey, Leicestershire
Printed and bound in Great Britain by
T. J. International Ltd., Padstow, Cornwall

This book is printed on acid-free paper

DEDICATION:
To the brave and dedicated men and women of the Philadelphia Police Department and to their former Public Relations Officer, Edward Tenuto.

Prologue

Sunday, June 30th, 1985

It was one of those dreams that seem so real. Tam was sitting at an outside table on some restaurant deck that overlooked a waterway. She held a scotch and soda in her hand; her son, David, drank an orange juice. Then David said he was going exploring in that underwater voice which dreams permit. He had gone off, climbing backwards down through some opening that led to an intermediate deck.

Then Asher Lowenstein appeared, leaning over the café table, the breeze ruffling his blond hair. Tam wondered why he was there and not busy working on some case for the Philadelphia Police Department.

'Don't worry,' Ash told her. 'I'm here and it's all right.'

She nodded, thinking of a dozen reasons for his concern and comfort.

Then a shot rang out and she moved ethereally to see its source.

And it wasn't all right, because David was dead, his stomach red with gunshot.

When she awoke, a sickly sensation engulfed her. She'd been psychic since the age of seventeen and for the past six months or so had been working at Asher's insistence with him and the police department. She'd recently located a young murder victim for them, more surprised than Ash that she'd accomplished anything at all. She felt uneasy at best going public with her talents, and picking up on a death on her first case had been traumatic.

The dream lurched her stomach — it had seemed too real. Like an aura of things to come; of prophecy. A bad prophecy.

She turned on the hallway light and peered into David's bedroom. He slept peacefully, his strong teenage body at repose. She switched off the light and climbed back into bed, troubled. Asher would tell her it was psychological, connected with the murder case she'd helped to solve. But until this dream faded, faded from memory, Tam would be haunted.

As she fell asleep, she thought again of telling Ash she wanted out. At least once a week she braced herself to admit she wasn't comfortable working with the Philadelphia Detective Bureau. And each time she let it go.

She couldn't say no to those who really needed her special brand of help.

* * *

SUMMER, 1944

The unaccustomed quiet of the house greeted him first. Then a grating, clicking sound. He moved cautiously, uneasy in the quiet, toward the phonograph where the needle skipped and skipped at the end of the 78 R.P.M. record. Lifting the needle, he turned the machine off, then put Ol' Blue Eyes back in his paper sleeve in the album cover. He'd just come back from the Bijou, watching James Cagney and Pat O'Brien in *The Fighting 69th* and wishing he was old enough to enlist. He wasn't even nine yet. By the time he grew up, the war would be over.

It was too quiet. It wasn't like her to leave her treasured record player on, wasting electricity. And even when she wasn't talking, she radiated sound, just like that tower in the beginning of the newsreel before the movie started. Dishes being scraped, house slippers shuffled, the scrub of floors or squeak of woodwork being washed, even the rustling pages of *The Ladies' Home Journal*, would fill the house.

Perhaps she was resting upstairs. The day was warm; too hot for heavy housework. He headed through the dining room to the kitchen, the icebox and cool ice water beckoning, hand on the swinging door between the rooms. No one could cook like her; he wondered what she'd make for dinner.

His hand froze. Sobs — muffled sobs; choking, snorting, out-of-control sobs — sounded from the kitchen. His fingers stuck to the wood; then slowly, feeling like a robot in those pulp science fiction mags his mother chided him for reading, he pushed the door wide open.

His mother lay on the floor, her mouth contorted, a large spray of blood wreathing her stomach: her pretty white apron with the ruffles, red; her freshly-scoured floor tiles, dotted with small puddles of red. His older brother, Tony, knelt weakly beside their mother, his trouser knees and legs saturated and red. A knife clasped in Tony's hands pointed upright, held as if in prayer too late for granting — the knife, red.

He watched the horror and fear on Tony's face, then felt his own stomach lurching at the scene before him. His rage grew.

'I didn't mean to, Walt,' Tony pleaded.

Walt stood, studying Tony, his body weighted down like stone. He hated his older brother.

Tony. Always trouble, always cantankerous, always fighting. Always no good. Mom always said so. He'd been no good ever since Dad got killed in the war.

Walt heard himself shouting, then

screaming. He felt as if he were the one aiming the furious diatribe at his brother — and yet outside himself, watching it all. Tony Buehl shrank back against the kitchen wall as if Walt's blistering words were lethal, scorching weapons, maiming him painfully.

The next-door neighbor, hearing the chaos, came, saw, and ran for the police. The responding officers found them, the tableau unchanged: Tony still cowering; Walter's shrill voice still resounding through the house. Over and over Walt shouted, his throat raw and hurting, but his words spewing from a fury that couldn't be stemmed. 'You're no good! You're a no good kid! You're a bad kid, a rotten kid, and you oughta be dead!'

Tony Buehl sank into the protective netherworld of insanity. He saw no more and heard no more that day. They led Tony to the squad car first, then gently began to steer Walter outside, too. He needed no prompting, following the retreating back of his older brother, making sure his words aimed straight and true for Tony's heart. Over and over again. They tried to calm him, but he screamed and shrieked out great scathing missives of hate, out of control.

'You oughta be dead! You oughta be dead! *YOU OUGHTA BE DEAD*!'

1

Tuesday, July 2nd, 1985

The delivery truck Tony Buehl had hidden himself in braked to a stop. Tony tensed his muscles to silence as the back door slid open. He could just about see the driver's shape flitting about the racks. He watched him consult his delivery roster and pull packages off the racks. Tony held his breath. The driver hopped down and disappeared into the grocery.

Tony sprang into action. He emerged from his camouflaged position, scattering fresh-baked loaves of bread off the rack in front of him and onto the truck floor. Grabbing donuts and cookies from another rack, he fled the truck.

He found himself on Bustleton Avenue, unfamiliar territory, and ran to the corner. Turning right on Tyson, Tony ran, his excitement surging, not stopping till he reached Roosevelt Boulevard.

He'd done it! He'd done it! He'd escaped from the hospital just like on TV. He hid in the truck and he didn't even have to sock out the driver like they did in that show. He'd thought of sneaking off the grounds at night, but was afraid he'd meet one of his guard friends. They'd make him feel foolish and make him go back to bed. Besides, the dark scared him. This was easier and not as scary. And fun! Tony liked this game and hoped Dr. Robbins wouldn't be too angry at him for leaving like that. He'd come back when he got tired of playing.

He stood near the traffic light and put out his thumb at the intersection to the drivers on the boulevard, just like on TV. One wave of cars passed, uncaring; but with the second wave, a horn honked from the blue station wagon three cars back, and a disheveled head of hair stuck itself out of the opened passenger-side window.

'Hey, my man, where you goin' with all that nutrition?'

Tony didn't understand about the nutrition but walked over to the car, wide-eyed. 'I need a ride.'

'Where you goin'?'

The man's beard and mustache parted to reveal a fleshy pink smile and fairly even teeth. With the mass of hair framing the rest of his face and the eyes twinkling under bushy brown brows, he looked like a young Santa Claus, and Tony felt comfortable telling the truth. 'I'm running away from home.'

'Far out!' the man said, and he swung the door open. 'Bein' I've got a massive hunger and you need some wheels, how 'bout you slide in here and we do some tradin'. Specially bein' the light's changin'.' He pointed at the traffic light, which shifted from red to green. Tony slid into the front seat and slammed the door. They took off down the boulevard.

Tony offered the cookies to the man, now wedged between a skinny long-haired blonde at the wheel and him.

'Far out, man! But I'd rather have the donuts.' Tony obliged him and he gingerly opened the package. 'This here's Claire.' He indicated the lanky blonde. 'And that's Murphy and Scrugs and Annie

10

Belle in the backseat.' Murphy looked like the oldest; wiry, tall and bald. Scrugs was small, Tony's size, with straight brown hair that seemed plastered to his head until it hung motionless at the top of his shoulders. Annie Belle was tiny and pretty with short brown hair that tapered around her ears, forehead and neck, and Tony blushed at her. She smiled back. He couldn't see much of Claire — the guy who looked like Santa Claus was, in fact, as big as Santa Claus. The donut box sat on his large belly, taking the bumps with it as the station wagon now avoided the potholes on its way out to the Schuylkill Expressway.

'My name's Tony,' he offered, feeling they were waiting to know.

'Far out!' the jovial, hairy fat guy answered, and Tony wondered if this guy knew John Denver. He had seen John Denver on TV and John Denver liked to say that. Tony went around a whole week saying, 'Far out!' until Dr. Robbins told him to say something different. Dr. Robbins had laughed and now this guy laughed, too. 'Far out, Tony! I was sittin'' here, thinkin', boy, I could do with some donuts, and there you were. Talk about creating out of the cosmic energy!' He held out his free hand. 'They call me Santa Ana.'

Tony shook his hand, a bubble of joy rising in his throat. He knew he was close. He couldn't resist asking the next question.

'Santa Ana?'

Santa Ana looked up from his munchies.

'Do you know Santa Claus?'

Everyone in the car roared. Tony hesitated, then joined in, feeling good.

'I don't know, man,' Santa Ana said, wiping mirthful tears from his eyes. 'Sometimes I think I'm one of his elves!'

'You look like him,' Tony said.

'You're funny,' Annie Belle offered from the backseat.

'Thank you,' Tony said, and he blushed.

'Tell you what, Tony,' Santa Ana said, 'why confuse things? Call me Santa. That's what they do.'

'Sure we do,' Scrugs added. 'But this guy's gonna expect presents under the tree at Christmas!'

Another round of laughter shot through the car and Tony joined in.

'Hey, Santa,' Murphy finally spoke, 'this guy's got no place to go and he's fun. Maybe he'd like to crash with us for a while.'

Claire, at the wheel, spoke. 'Tony seems nice but I'd like to know what he's runnin' from.' She leaned forward as she spoke, and Tony saw a thin but pretty face and slightly wavy hair that curled at the base of her neck.

Santa turned to him. 'Well, Tony?'

Tony shrugged, uncomfortable. 'They locked me up. My brother, Walt, he won't let me out. Dr. Robbins said I could get out but Walt won't let me. So I ran away from home.' He looked at them imploringly. 'I won't be any trouble. I just wanted to get away a little. I won't be no trouble, please.' When they didn't answer, he added, 'I been locked up a long time and Walt won't let me out.'

The whole carload seemed to galvanize into action.

'You can stay with us, man,' Santa

muttered. 'We've got room at our house in Germantown. Far out, man! Someone lockin' up a nice little guy like you!'

'We'll protect you,' Claire said firmly. 'Don't worry about that brother of yours.'

'It's fine with us,' Murphy said from the back, and Scrugs and Annie Belle nodded.

'Don't you worry, Tony.' Annie Belle laid a tender hand on his shoulder. 'We're your family now.'

Tony turned to her, a shy, grateful smile on his face. 'Thank you very much.' She smiled back and his own smile broke even wider.

'Far out!' he laughed and everyone hugged their sides and bellies, even Claire at the wheel.

All this, Tony thought, and Christmas, too.

★   ★   ★

The house at 837 Coulter Street was two-storied with high ceilings. It had, Tony discovered, three large bedrooms, and he was assigned to sleep in the

14

middle one with Scrugs, Scrugs currently having no girlfriend. Tony told him he didn't have a girl, either, so Scrugs wouldn't feel bad.

'Hey, man, you're not funny, are you?' Scrugs asked cautiously as he showed him the room.

Tony looked puzzled. 'Well, you guys thought I was funny in the car.'

Scrugs's eyebrows shot up, then he broke into a wide grin and a short laugh. 'You're a riot. I mean gay.'

Tony thought. 'Well, I'm happy some of the time.'

Scrugs scratched his cocked head in a mind-boggled manner. 'How long have you been locked up, man?'

There was definite reluctance on Tony's part to say. Then he answered, simply, 'Well, I turned twelve the first year. I remember turning twelve and feeling all alone.' Sorrow echoed his words from the resurgence of a memory he'd thought he'd forgotten, and he turned his head away from Scrugs to hide from the hurt.

'Man,' Scrugs said, standing in the deathly hush, 'that brother of yours must've been a bastard.'

'Walt . . . ' Tony began, then stopped.

Scrugs freed the silence. 'You don't have to talk about it, if you don't want to.'

'I don't wanta talk about it,' Tony said.

'Fine. Look. You're gonna need some clothes since you took off from your loony bin brother's place. I guess you can't go back and sneak some clothes out, can you?'

'No. Dr. Robbins would make me stay there.'

'I thought this doctor dude was on your side?'

'He is. He told me so. But Walt's my brother and he's gotta do what Walt says.' His face still drooped from depression.

'Hell, man. You can use my clothes. I got some extra.' He studied Tony's small frame. 'Yeah, we're about the same.'

Tony fidgeted sheepishly. 'You sure? I feel like I'm makin' trouble for you. I can just wear these clothes.' He looked down at his plain blue work shirt and jeans.

'Nah, you're no trouble. You gotta wash 'em sometimes. Look, Tony, I know what it's like bein' down and out. I been there.

Fact is, if it wasn't for Santa Ana, I'd still be there. I got friends now. You got friends, too.'

Scrugs held out his hand. Tony, touched and grateful, met it slowly with his own. They squeezed and shook.

Hands parted.

'Thanks,' Tony said, feeling for the first time in forty-one years a strange sense of freedom and independence. He looked at the younger man, tasting the feel of the words '*You got friends,*' over again in his mind. 'I'm glad.'

Scrugs smiled. He looked to Tony like the little guy from The Lollipop Guild from *The Wizard of Oz*, except for having hair.

Annie Belle stuck her head around the doorway. 'Hey, you guys,' she smiled, 'chow's on.' She disappeared daintily into the hallway and down the stairs.

'She's a doll,' Scrugs said, admiring her, 'but she's Murphy's woman. They're a solid item. You know what I mean?'

'That's nice.' Tony smiled. He liked Annie Belle, too. That Murphy was a lucky guy.

* * *

Santa Ana, Claire and Murphy had been fast friends since the late sixties. Murphy had known Scrugs from his old Kensington neighborhood and was just dating Annie Belle in 1980 when Santa and Claire decided to buy the rambling house in Germantown. Murphy and Annie Belle moved in with them and Scrugs came a year later. Santa jokingly called them a commune but what they had was indeed a communal family, their interests and philosophies remarkably compatible. They were loyal to New Age ideals, especially truth, which was the cornerstone of their beliefs. There was no truth, they solemnly told Tony, that didn't have a greater truth behind it. For truth was not a goal you reached, but constantly traveled to.

'It's like school, man,' Santa Ana intoned as they sat at dinner, 'you never stop learning. But it's the school of life. And love . . . love is your schoolbook because it's like in relationships we learn to get along with each other.' He swirled a

18

huge fork load of spaghetti and chewed and swallowed thoughtfully. 'Love is gonna save the world.'

Claire rested her own fork gently on her plate. 'Tony, why'd your brother lock you up?' She sat at quiet attention as if that statement summed up all the world's indignities.

Tony immediately felt his stomach harden; it tightened like a rock. All ten eyes were on him and it didn't help that they thought he'd been hurt. 'I — ' he began. 'I — done something bad.'

When he didn't continue, Claire gestured encouragingly with her hand. 'What?'

Tony had the sensation of being trapped.

Scrugs, across from him, reacted to the terror on Tony's face. 'Hey, man, he doesn't want to talk about it.'

Annie Belle jumped in. 'You don't have to tell us, Tony. It was long ago, anyway, wasn't it? A person shouldn't be penalized forever for an error.' She addressed the group. 'I sense a goodness in Tony, a childlike spirit that's been wronged by a

19

judgment harsher than whatever act of wrongdoing he committed.' She turned to Tony. 'Are my feelings right?'

Tony slowly shook his head, surprising the group. 'You're all so good to me.' Tears began to cascade down his cheeks, then his face screwed up, wreathed in grief. His great bitterness seared them as he spoke. 'I killed my mother. I didn't mean to. It was an accident. We were angry. Oh,' he clutched his stomach, tears flowing endlessly, as he bowed his head, 'I didn't want to remember it!'

As the chill left and the shock began to dissipate, Claire asked in a thin, agonized voice, 'Tony, how old were you?'

The bowed head didn't lift. The small shoulders heaved from ongoing sobs. 'Eleven,' he muttered weakly.

The confession had been sparked; he could not stop the desolate sorrow surging up at long last in a continuous salty river, pain coursing up his muscles as the confession of his guilt released his long-repressed feelings of remorse. And his great need to bring his mother back.

Santa Ana took command of the

situation. He left his chair and knelt beside Tony. 'Is that when they locked you up, man?'

Tony nodded his head, not looking up. 'Dr. Robbins said I was okay now, that I wouldn't hurt no one. I never meant to hurt no one. Not Mama!'

A fiercer spasm of tears wrenched him. When he surfaced from the fresh emotional storm, he said, 'It don't matter what Dr. Robbins says. Walt's gonna make me stay locked up forever. Cause I deserve it.' He succumbed to another hard-breaking wave; the sobs wracked his body so hard, he hit his lowered head against the table's edge. He took in the physical shock, then continued crying.

'No!' Annie Belle said, forcibly. 'You've been punished enough. I was right! We'll protect you. We'll protect you forever, if necessary.'

Claire came over and put her hand soothingly on Tony's shoulder. 'I sense what you say,' she seconded Annie Belle. 'I know that you're right.'

Murphy, stoical in his chair, offered a quiet stony comment. 'Long time to pay for a stupid, bad mistake. Your brother's no good.'

Tony's eyes flew open. He raised his head and looked at Murphy. But Murphy's face softened in sympathy. Tony shut his eyes as the pain returned, but caught Scrugs's face, matching his in its sorrow.

'I sense,' said Santa Ana gravely, 'a very lonely soul come home. To start again.'

★ ★ ★

The women coddled and babied Tony until his tremors and his aching passed and he was able to sleep. They left him resting on the small cot in Scrugs's room, and retired to Santa Ana and Claire's small back bedroom to discuss the turn of events. They decided he was truly a lost soul whose suffering was complete. The vote was unanimous; they would trust him and protect him. They would let Tony stay with them, be a part of their family.

Murphy and Annie Belle retired to their front bedroom. Scrugs said good-night and returned to his own. He looked at Tony, sleeping peacefully at last, then turned off the light. He stripped down to his underwear and, getting into bed, listened intently in the darkness. Reassured by the even sound of breathing across the room, he fell asleep.

★　★　★

'Tony . . . put the gun down. Slowly.'

'It's not real, is it?' Tony held the small pistol this way and that, his finger curling lightly around the trigger.

'Tony . . . put it down . . . now. Real gently.'

Tony laid the gun back in the drawer he'd discovered it in. 'Is it real?' he asked, his face tinged with wonder.

'Nah, I just use it to play cowboys and Indians.' Scrugs rolled his eyes. 'Listen, Tony, you're not allowed to touch that gun again. You understand?'

'Why, if it's not for real?'

'Cause it's for bad guys,' Scrugs intoned.

'To protect me?'

'Yeah, to protect you. So don't go

playing with it. Okay?'

'Okay.' Tony slowly shut the drawer, his eyes on the gun.

'What were you doin' messin' in the drawers anyway?'

'Just lookin'. You said I could share your clothes. I was just curious.'

'Too curious,' Scrugs said testily. 'Didn't you hear that killed the cat?'

Tony's mouth fell; he wondered if Scrugs was putting him on. 'Someone killed a cat with that gun?'

Scrugs's face scrunched up and he fell into a fit of laughter.

'And dumb, too,' he added, wiping his moistened eyes. 'Tony, just don't go messin' with that thing. You could hurt yourself or somebody.'

Tony nodded but silently wondered why Scrugs wouldn't share his toy. If it wasn't real, why couldn't he play with it?

2

Thursday, July 4th

Tony finished tucking in the new shirt
Scrugs had given him. It was neat; it
looked like a cowboy's shirt with its fancy
stitching. Boy, he could really be a
cowboy in this shirt. All he needed was a
holster and a gun.

'Come on, Tony,' Scrugs shouted from
downstairs. Tony glanced at the closed
drawer with its forbidden contents.

'I'm coming,' he shouted. 'Just a minute!'
He grabbed the denim jacket Scrugs had
loaned him and put it on. His eyes riveted
over to the drawer again. Scrugs was downstairs. He could just hold the gun for a
minute and put it right back.

He opened the drawer and lifted the
gun out. He struck a cowboy stance,
pretending.

'Come on, Tony!' Scrugs was ascending
the stairs.

Panicking, Tony shut the drawer, only to realize he still held the gun. He heard Scrugs reach the landing.

'Are you ready or are we gonna have to stand a mile back to see the Beach Boys?'

'I'm ready,' Tony said, and followed Scrugs compliantly downstairs, his hands in the wide jacket pockets. He couldn't let Scrugs know he'd broken his promise. He'd have to wait till later now to put it back.

One hand clutched the gun tightly within.

* * *

Claire was an avid shopper and Annie loved water because it flowed to the sea. Claire, because of a trust fund set up by a generous eccentric father, had a sizeable stipend to draw from every month. Most of it went to maintaining their needs; enough remained for her to shower small trinkets on herself and her friends. Annie considered herself psychic, tuned into the cosmic awareness, and viewed all rivers as mystical. They only needed to hear, therefore, that Tony had never seen Penn's Landing or the new revitalized South Street, for Annie to insist he should take in the energetic vibrations of the colorful waterfront and Claire to decide Tony should be treated to a stroll along the famed South Street shops.

Although the tall ships hadn't arrived, there was a multitude of small craft hugging the docks and traversing the waterways, in high anticipation of Independence Day celebrations. Tony ran along the Landing like an adolescent, drawing cock-eyed stares from some passers-by while his friends enjoyed his unrestrained pleasure at the festival atmosphere around him.

'You're catching the vibrations, Tony,' Annie Belle shouted over to him. 'Isn't it like rejuvenating?'

'Independence Day. That means freedom.' Tony grinned. 'I remember that from the man on TV.' He mimicked: ''Independence Day. The day we celebrate our country's freedom.'' He quieted. 'Now I'm free.'

Tourists and natives milled past them.

The look on the faces of his new friends reminded him of his mother's face when he'd said something especially pleasing to her.

'Free as a bird.' Santa Ana grinned back and, draping an enormous arm around Tony's back and shoulder, gave him a shake that nearly lifted him off the ground.

Colorful food vendors dotted the waterfront, situated temptingly around the pavilions, the Port of History Museum, the grassy landscaped knolls that angled down to the Landing's walkways and the Delaware River. The day was heady with sunlight, fair breezes and just the right caress of warmth. The six friends ambled along. They met the day with a youthful enthusiasm never surrendered to something so blatantly mortal as a mere passage of years.

Annie Belle, the youngest, was twenty-eight. Scrugs was thirty-two. Claire, thirty-eight, and Santa Ana, forty-two, were the only married members of the group. They had met at a concert at the Spectrum one Saturday night three months after her father's death. A whirlwind courtship followed and they were married by a judge two months later. After the others joined them at the house on Coulter Street, Annie Belle held a candlelight ceremony for them, at which she officiated — a special ceremony, she said, which would link their love more purely with the universe. Murphy, forty-six, also had no faith in legal contracts, but any passer-by could see he loved his Annie and was fiercely protective toward her. She returned his loyalty two-fold but opted against vows. Her energy had to be free, she insisted, to take in the vibrations of the cosmic universe. Murphy treated her like his Oracle of Delphi whose wisdom was his sacred trust. They held hands tightly now, a line of tension rippling the muscle in Murphy's arm as other men gave Annie's pert face and figure appreciative side glances. Scrugs, Tony, Claire and Santa Ana tripped along light-heartedly beside them, Santa's solid bulk no barrier to the soaring spirit of the day.

Tony, while enjoying the scene, grew

hungrier at the sight of each vendor they passed. 'Candy apples!' He pointed, unable to stand it any longer.

'Save your appetite,' Claire said, smiling at his still pointed finger. 'We're going to eat on South Street. They've got some great pizza at this little shop on Fourth Street.'

'But I'd rather get an apple.' His arm slowly lowered to his side.

'Be good, Tony. I'll treat you to some ice cream for dessert.'

The thought of ice cream made his mouth water. He wondered if they'd have chocolate fudge ripple. 'Okay.'

'You're easy, Tony,' Scrugs laughed.

They chuckled at his eagerness and headed out of Penn's Landing, through the shopping and restaurant complex of New Market, and out to Second Street which, one block down, met with South.

* * *

They didn't have chocolate fudge ripple but they had something even better: chocolate raspberry truffle. It had nuts in it, too, and Tony licked at it happily as they trotted along South Street. It wasn't long before he was down to the cone. And then that disappeared, Tony savoring the last crunch and swallow.

'Boy, that was fast!' Claire said, still working on her mint chocolate chip.

Everyone but Murphy was enjoying an ice cream cone, Santa's a double-decker. Tony had put that pleasure behind him now, relishing the new pleasure of walking unhampered on this vivid city street. And what sights to see. Stores filled with fun things, wonderful things. Book stores, furniture stores, fancy grocery stores that showed delicious cakes and candies and other mouth-watering treats beyond their clear shop windows. Clothing boutiques and record stores with posters. And open-air vendors at each intersection selling jewelry, handbags and a large array of other goods.

'Oh, look!' One vendor's display of earrings, sunlight casting fiery rays upon them, caught Claire's attention. She and Annie converged upon the dealer's packed table to inspect the dangling variety of gold and silver electroplate and semiprecious and simulated gems. The men waited patiently on the corner of Fourth and South, long used to Claire's passion for trinkets. Murphy walked over, at Annie's call, to help her make a selection. She modeled them against her ears for him coquettishly.

Tony watched, mesmerized by the gleam of the metal and stones, caught up in their shiny beauty for some minutes. Then he turned his head to gaze at South Street, taking in the vibrant crowd of people coming and going.

Suddenly his gaze froze on one man walking toward them.

No, it couldn't be!

Tony bolted and was on the other side of South Street before Santa Ana and Scrugs could react.

'Tony!'

He heard Santa shout his name but he couldn't stop. He ran fearfully along Fourth Street, turning down two side streets before his panic subsided and the throbbing ache in his side slowed him down. He knew he was lost and his legs felt like jelly, but his eyes searched, head darting nervously around for the face he had seen.

How would he ever find his friends?

What if his brother Walt had seen him, too?

Was Walt walking these streets, looking for him now?

Tony felt inside his pocket and wrapped his hand around the gun. Maybe it was a toy but if Walt came to get him, to lock him up, Walt wouldn't know that. He might scare Walt away.

He walked on, feeling faint, not knowing where he was heading, trying to find Claire and Scrugs and the others. His heart beat fast and his hand tightened on the firearm in his pocket. It gave him small comfort.

★ ★ ★

They found him on the corner of Sixth and Catherine. Murphy and Annie Belle had gone in one direction searching; Claire, Santa Ana and Scrugs in another. Scrugs spotted him first, his back turned to them, as they traveled down Sixth Street. 'Tony!'

Tony's small figure pivoted sharply, a look of fear on his face. Then, seeing Scrugs with Claire and Santa, a wave of relief washed over his features. They drew closer to him. He walked weakly over to them.

'Man,' Scrugs said, seeing Tony's wobbly gait, 'you're shaking. Are you sick?'

'I think I'm gonna be.'

Then Scrugs noticed the hole in the pocket of the blue denim jacket and the flash of silver peeking through it.

'What's in the pocket, Tony?'

Tony slowly took out the gun. His hand quivered as he gave it to Scrugs. Scrugs took it quickly and placed it in his own pocket.

'I told you not to take that, Tony!'

'I was gonna put it back. I was just gonna play with it a minute, then you came into the room before I could put it back.' He stared at Scrugs, sour-lipped. 'You shoulda told me it was real!'

A sharp intake of breath from Claire

punctuated their shock, their pin-drop silence. Tony lowered his head, eyes cast down to avoid theirs.

'How didya know it was real, Tony?' Scrugs asked. 'And where'd this come from?' He fingered the small hole in Tony's pocket.

Annie Belle, walking down Catherine Street with Murphy, spotted Tony and the others. Claire, seeing their approach, walked over and explained in a whisper.

'Well,' Tony began.

'Well, what?' Scrugs asked.

Tony hesitated. 'Well, I was holding the gun in my pocket, because I was scared. I was holding it real tight with my finger on the trigger. And it went off.' He paused, blanched, then added, 'It really scared me.'

Santa finally spoke up, quietly. 'Where did the bullet go?'

Tony suddenly became more animated. 'Come on! I'll show you!' He walked them down Catherine and across Seventh Street. They stood in a dirt-filled lot with a few cars parked in it. Tony's eyes scanned the dirt and he walked slowly over to one spot between the cars. 'Here.' They searched the yellowed mounds of earth but no bullet could be found.

'You're sure it went off here?' Santa asked, his heavy bulk seemingly weighted by the solemn turn of events.

'Yeah.' Tony looked at them helplessly. 'I don't know where it went to. It should've went right there.' He pointed to an area they'd already combed.

'All right, Tony,' Santa said, 'what's done is done. What were you scared of, anyway?'

'I thought I saw Walt.'

'Your brother?' Annie Belle asked, and her mouth set in a hard line. Her eyes questioned the wisdom of remaining in South Philadelphia.

Murphy took charge. 'Come on. Let's get back to Penn's Landing and get the car. The concert's gonna start pretty soon.'

They walked quickly down Catherine Street to Third, up Third to Chestnut, then down Chestnut to the Landing. Tony moved stiffly, afraid that at any moment

36

Walt would appear and confront him.

In the car, on their way to find a parking spot near the Parkway, Tony sat still and rigid in the back seat with Murphy and Annie. Murphy slapped Tony's knee in a lively manner. 'Loosen up, man. You're like a wooden Indian.'

'I'm still scared.'

'Man, that crowd'll be so thick, you won't be able to see no one.'

'That's right!' Claire said suddenly. 'Tony, we don't want you getting lost again . . . or getting into trouble. Annie, you hold his hand when we get to the Parkway, and Tony . . . don't you let go!'

Tony's mouth dropped open with surprise at Claire's instructions. Then a little smile crept up at the corners. He leaned back in a more relaxed position. Murphy, who'd be holding Annie's other dainty hand, checked out Tony's loose posture and shy grin and laughed.

★ ★ ★

Mrs. Anna Gambetti would never forget that particular Thursday: the Fourth of July, 1985. She had hoped for some peace on that day, a holiday, a day off from the dry cleaners where she worked on Christian Street. The South Philadelphia streets were hot and the fans in the two-bedroom apartment on 7th Street only gave out a small breeze, enough to keep her moving, preparing dinner for herself and her son. Her fingers worked some kinks out of her brown perm as Nicky continued to plague her about the concert on the parkway.

'The Beach Boys, Mom! The whole world is down there right now, and the guys are waiting for me. Come on, Mom, just five bucks!'

'The money ain't the problem.' She felt her lips pursing tight in anger, the heat and frustration getting to her. 'You could get trampled down there. I saw it on the TV. It's a mob.'

'It's just people, Momma. Havin' a good time.'

'Somebody got arrested. I saw it on the TV.'

'To hell with it!' Nicky spat and grabbed her pocketbook, opening it.

Anna lunged for it. Her hand tightened on the shoulder strap as Nicky jerked it violently in his direction. The leather stretched and tore. 'Now, look what you done! You broke my purse!' Anna's injured tone launched itself like a dagger at her son. Nicky busied himself, pulling out her wallet, taking the five.

He threw the ruined handbag back at her. 'I'm sick of you babying me. Ever since Dad died, you're afraid to let me cross the street.'

He left the kitchen, silent in his fury now, heading for the front door.

Anna slowly turned off the gas burners. She moved dully toward her bedroom, clutching her broken purse.

New cursing erupted suddenly, filtering through from the living room. 'God Almighty, Mom, I'm fifteen. And I'm going to the concert whether you like it or not. So go to hell!'

She waited, lost in a mindless vacuum

of despair, for the sharp slam. This was the worst, the worst he had ever done. It all piled on her: his bad grades, his cutting school, the vulgarity and disrespect whenever he couldn't get his way. She didn't mean to be possessive; he just was all she had. She didn't want to lose him, like Frank, five years ago.

She heard the front door open, then silence, then the sound of steps coming toward her. Nicky stood in the bedroom doorway.

'I'm sorry,' he said, his tone sullen. His eyes fell on the pocketbook. 'But I'm going.'

Anna lifted the pocketbook like a cross. 'Look what you did! You're no good! You're killing me!'

He turned his back on her and walked out of the room.

Anna followed him to the bedroom doorway. 'You're no good!' she screamed after him, her anger coiling up within her. She retreated back to the bed, empty and lost again, and sat limply, sure he would meet with no good in that huge, unruly crowd. A boy always looking for trouble, her Nicky. She always said that, and didn't he always prove her right?

She heard a curious popping sound. The potatoes? Didn't she turn that gas range off? She jumped to her feet, heading into the kitchen. Hurrying, from the corner of her eye, she caught the top of the front door. Wide open. Stupid kid went out and left the place wide open.

The burners were off; she had turned them off — the popping sound must've come from outside. Leaving the kitchen to close the front door, she moved across the living room. Halfway across, her breath caught in her throat.

'Nicky?' she whispered. He was stretched out on his stomach on the rug, half-in, half-out of the apartment. 'Nicky? You hurt?'

She started to turn him. He must've tripped and fallen and hit his head. Her hand, trying to pull him around, felt the oozing warmth. Panicking, pulling him onto his back, she saw the spurting red spreading, spreading, dying his white tee shirt, leaping from his chest to the rug.

Anna Gambetti screamed and screamed and screamed.

Nicky! Nicky! Always looking for trouble!

But there weren't any troubles left for Nicky Gambetti to find.

3

Saturday, July 6th

For Tam, it was another boring Saturday night in Philadelphia. She was thirty-six and had forgotten what a date was. Since her second divorce — new and damning evidence that she chose marriage partners with the finesse of a bad interior decorator clashing colors — her sparkle and her life had suddenly fizzled. She had signed up at two agencies, working assignments as a temporary secretary to supplement the child support payments she received from Daniel, her first husband. At least something good had come from that union. But now that she was in between assignments, money was tight and pleasures simple. So she sat, listening to the 'Saturday Nite Oldies Show' on WMGK and playing a losing battle at cards with David, her thirteen-year-old son.

'I'm out,' David gloated, holding up three aces, top winners in a round that racked him up a hundred-plus points.

'You win,' Tam conceded. 'You're well over 500.'

The radio blurted out some Beatles, then the Temps, then threw in that current rapping noise Tam couldn't stomach. During their game she had surprised herself, swaying to the sixties music. But now, game over, the radio bopped forward in time to the Eighties with its curious mix of soft rock, hard rock and philanthropy. Tam felt once again like E.T. She contemplated a cooling bath and bed.

The telephone rang. David picked it up gingerly, talked for five minutes then handing her the phone. 'It's for you.'

'If it's for me, why didn't you tell me? Who is it?'

'Ash.'

'Oh,' Tam said, but David had gone in the direction of the bathroom. She wondered why Ash was calling on a Saturday night, a bachelor with a nice combination of blond good looks and quiet sophistication. She spoke into the phone. 'Hi.'

'Tammy, darling.' Asher's voice rumbled through evenly with just the right amount of gravel, both a turn-on and irksome. 'I need you.'

'Personally or professionally?' she asked, then laughed.

He laughed back. 'Which do you prefer?' But an edge of concern crept in. 'Still down in the dumps over Bill?'

'Getting over it.'

His tone dropped down, serious. 'I need you on a case.'

He gave her the details over the phone.

★ ★ ★

'Mrs. Gambetti?'

Asher Lowenstein walked toward the glassy-eyed woman. She was seated on one of the black vinyl-padded benches that flanked the miniscule entrance to Homicide. Tam Westington followed quietly behind him.

'Thank you for coming down to Headquarters again. This is Tamara

45

Westington. She's a psychic working with us at Homicide.'

Anna Gambetti looked up at him imploringly. Her gaze met with sensitive brown eyes, a slightly rounded nose, and a small but generous mouth above a cleft chin. His thick sandy hair was neatly in place, his summer suit smooth and unwrinkled. 'Lieutenant Lowenstein, I told you before. I didn't do it. We were fighting, Nicky and me, but I wouldn't kill my boy.'

'Nobody said you did, Mrs. Gambetti,' Asher soothed her.

'But that Sergeant Colby, when I came down here the first time, kept saying how there was nobody there but me and Nicky and there was no witnesses and we were fighting. And Captain Anunzio told me I couldn't leave the city and now you tell me to come down here again. But I didn't do it. I didn't kill my Nicky.' She lowered her face and cast her eyes down, locked in a netherworld of grief.

Ash knelt until he was level with the woman sitting slumped and clutching the seam of the vinyl cushion tightly.

'I asked you here to help us . . . to help us find whoever killed Nicky.'

The woman's gaze lifted. 'Yeah?'

'Yeah. Did you bring some threads from the carpet like I asked you?'

'Yeah.' She fumbled in her purse and brought out a small packet of wrapped tissues. Timidly, she handed it to him.

'These were from the part of the carpet Nicky was lying on?'

'Yeah.' The woman nodded, her hand trying to smooth her disheveled permanent. 'Them police lab people came also and took samples and stuff. But these they didn't touch. I found them behind the lamp that's near the door.'

Asher opened up the tissues. Three light brown threads, crusted with drops of blood, greeted him. 'This is fine, Mrs. Gambetti.' He stood up.

'You think you're gonna catch the killer?' She had quietly begun to cry, her face passive, her next words bitter. 'Nobody saw nothin'.'

'We're going to do our best, Mrs. Gambetti.' He hated the redundant line. It always sounded departmental, no matter how sincerely he spoke it.

'No witnesses,' the woman repeated in a murmur, her gaze questioning him.

'That's why I've called Ms. Westington in on the case. She was fairly accurate in locating a murder victim a few months ago.'

'A psychic,' Mrs. Gambetti sniffed, as if uncertain how to view Tam — charlatan or prospective saint. She clutched her rosary for protection's sake and stared bluntly at Tam, taking in her Shirley Temple looks, golden locks dangling at her neck, the small nose, wide blue eyes, and the elfin features. Young, but not too young: tiny crow lines at the eyes. 'Murder victims, huh? Let's see how she does with murderers.'

Mrs. Gambetti got up sullenly to leave, but shot a quick parting glance at Tam. It seemed to say she hoped Tam proved a saint.

* * *

'I'm not up to this,' Tam said. 'That boy wasn't much older than David.'

Asher studied the petite blonde psychic he'd shared close friendship with for over ten years and was now working with on blind cases. It had been tough convincing her to use her talents to aid the Philadelphia Detective Bureau.

She caught his stare. 'Do I look that bad?'

'You went through a divorce, not the end of your life.' She sat down at a parallel desk, her tightly balled fist against her cheek as she leaned on her elbow, and so he answered her directly. 'You look fine.'

'No, I don't. I gained fifteen pounds since the marriage and five more dissolving it.'

'Okay,' he said, 'so you're feeling sorry for yourself. We can talk about that later. In the meantime, I have paperwork to review and a murder to solve.' He sat down nonchalantly at his desk and opened the file on the Gambetti case, rechecking the interviews with the neighbors, the case history on the mother, the murdered son, and the statement taken from the mother. The reports basically matched. Only the language varied: the sounds of the fight between mother and son, the muffled popping sound, the sound of something falling hard which the man in the next apartment heard but the distraught mother didn't; and then Mrs. Gambetti's screams — freezing the timid ones, calling forth the hardier ones within earshot. The Medical Examiner's Office estimated the timing of the murder to be minutes, maybe five at most, before the body was discovered. The killer had been quick and cautious, timing himself into pure invisibility. And as far as motive, nothing yet. Nicky Gambetti hadn't been in any gang; if anything, he'd been a loner, mixing poorly with his own age group. His few friends had been cocky stand-outs, too, somehow not cool enough to fit into any accepted group, upper class or low. Ash, along with Dennis Colby, had talked to these kids at school; they were harmless and scared. Murder was out of their league. No, it hadn't been a case of teenage vendetta. And teenage killers didn't cover their tracks that well.

He shut the files and leaned back to stretch and caught Tam's sulky glance. He decided to ignore it and reached for the ballistics report.

'Am I that wrapped up in self-pity? Does it come off like that, Ash? Does it show like some rotten disease that disfigures the facial features?'

He didn't look up from the paperwork. 'You look fine. I might even say adorable if you perked up. Go look in the mirror in the women's room. See for yourself.'

'Asher . . . '

His head lifted abruptly. 'Dammit, Tammy, he used a Saturday Night Special, a handgun anyone can buy, and was close enough for an accurate shot to the heart. And he got away clean — no trace, no suspicious character noted in the neighborhood. At least, no one anyone remembered. That means he fit in, caused no heads to turn. He could be anyone, this joker who murdered a fifteen-year-old boy with no apparent motive.' He caught his angry breath, controlled himself, and forced his tone down a notch or two. 'Now I know you're going through changes, but if your head is too muddled to help on this case, tell me and I'll send you on your way. Because I've got to answer to Anunzio on this case and my shoulder just isn't available to you emotionally tonight.'

Tam bristled. 'I'm not feeling very good at it tonight. Maybe I will go home — tomorrow will be better.'

'Tammy, wait.' He handed her the small tissue-wrapped package. 'Take the rug samples with you. When you're feeling better, maybe you can concentrate and get something. I'm sorry I laid into you like that.'

She took the package from his out-stretched hand. She started to answer him, feeling foolish, when a loud and deliberate sound of someone clearing his throat made them realize they'd been overheard.

Captain Frank Anunzio emerged from his office majestically, his barrel chest preceding him in the dignified manner of a man used to ruling his roost.

'Well, Lieutenant Lowenstein, I've heard of sexual abuse, psychological abuse, physical abuse and child abuse.

Are you coining a new term called psychic abuse? Is he being too hard on you, my dear?'

'No, Captain.' Tam gave her head, and subsequently her curls, a minute shake. 'I deserved it.'

'A classic syndrome, my dear.' Captain Anunzio put his arm lightly around her. 'The victim thinks she caused the abuse by some imagined wrong committed.'

Ash let a furtive sigh escape, realizing he'd been holding his breath. 'I apologized to the lady, Captain.'

'And well you should.' Anunzio's carefully manicured crew cut seemed to stand up even straighter in stiff brown waves, in keeping with his moral lecture. 'He gets too wrapped up in his work,' he said, confidentially, paternally, his brown eyes on Tam, his powerful chin jerking toward Asher.

'He's a good detective,' Tam said unexpectedly, feeling she must defend Ash against the Captain. 'It was nice of you to be concerned, Captain, but, really, I'm all right. I'm going to take these rug samples home — ' she held up the packet as if to

53

cement her intentions — 'and see if I can get anything from them. I'll give you a call, Ash.' She grabbed her pocketbook from where she had slung it over a nearby chair and left without a backward glance.

Frank Anunzio leaned over the desk and looked squarely into Asher's steady eyes. 'For God's sake, man,' he murmured, 'if you're going to chew her out, lower your voice. You could be heard two offices down.' He straightened himself slowly, walked back to his office and closed the door behind him.

Ash shut his eyes in an exasperated gesture, then opened them and returned to the paperwork, reading it over and over, searching for the loophole in the facts that could lead him to a viable motive for the murder of Nicky Gambetti.

* * *

Sunday morning, July 7th, 12:30 A.M.

Tam stared at the rug samples wrapped pristinely in the white tissues. She had removed them from her handbag five minutes ago after David had dozed off on the couch, too drowsy to fight sleep. Tam had turned off *Saturday Night Live* and listened to the crickets take over the silence outside her first floor apartment in a countrified section of Oxford Circle. She was glad she'd found this place in the Northeast with as much grass and gardens as cement and brick. David could walk to Fels Junior High and Tam had the peace and quiet, though not a big point with David, that psychic work called for.

She remembered her first case with the Homicide Division — to locate a young girl abducted from a schoolyard by a relative. The relative swore he'd dropped the girl off at home that day. The child had been missing one week when Asher asked Tam — pleaded with her — to help. He had brought her down to Headquarters, given her the doll the child had dropped during the abduction, and filled her in on all the pertinent details of the case.

The other detectives had been skeptical of Tam's talents; some were visibly hostile at Asher's open though unofficial use of a psychic. Captain Anunzio had asked her bluntly what she charged. She didn't, she told him, surprising him. If she helped out at all, the good captain could make a charitable donation to any organization of his choice, to help another person, if he chose to do so. That would be payment enough.

The word spread that Tam was sincere, if nothing else. The detective bullpen sat back smugly to see if Asher's lady friend could prove her stuff with hard evidence. And the psychic clues Tam came up with, clues she herself couldn't link together, led the police to a remote wooded area in New Jersey. The hardest part was having to tell Asher the child was dead. She cried as she told him this, her emotions wracking her body. She described the manner of death as if needing to unburden herself of the terrible vision.

Homicide worked in concert with New Jersey authorities and the F.B.I. They found the child, dead a week and a half. Asher had given her ample time to recuperate, as shaken as she was by the gruesome case, and shocked by her ability to help. She had secretly hoped he never called her on another case again. In her other psychic work, conducted in her spare time as people came to her in need of her talents, Tam probed and gave advice — helping them to understand themselves and the potentials and probabilities in their lives, to make decisions, to be more hopeful and stronger in facing their present and their future.

But police work, as she thus far saw it, was not preventative. A crime was committed; it had to be solved. A psychic only helped to piece it together. Perhaps, Tam thought, the bottom line here was preventing the criminal from further acts of violence. Yet, neither this nor the new respect and acceptance she now received from Homicide could make up for the razor chills she got from probing psychically into a murder.

And now Ash had given her the new case of a murdered teenage boy. And she wanted to help — help find the person who committed this atrocity. For the police. For the mother who'd lost a son.

They needed her help; she would give them her best effort.

Tam looked at her sleeping tow-headed son and thought of Nicky Gambetti lying cold in the morgue. This was going to be hard. Facts, she reminded herself; you're going for facts. She undid the tissues and removed the stained strands of rug. Cupping them in her hands, she dimmed the lighting in her dining room and sat at the table in a comfortable position. She shut her eyes and breathed, inhaling slowly, exhaling slowly. She did it once, twice, three times, then allowed her breath to come naturally, with conscious control.

She blanked her mind, except for the repetition of the mantra, 'Om,' mentally saying it in concert with each of her breaths. Images, thoughts, ordinary worries and concerns snuck into her mind. She acknowledged each renegade thought, then banished it by repeating the 'Om,' concentrating on its lulling sound. Soon the stray thoughts left. Tam concentrated her attention on the blank void before her, shifting shades of dark and light behind her closed lids, then centered her awareness on the existence and feel of the rug samples in her hand.

She felt a heaviness, a sleepiness, descend upon her, and felt herself drifting off, while still sitting upright yet relaxed in the chair. An image flashed in the darkness. James Cagney. James Cagney, *Yankee Doodle Dandy*, thought Tam, and she frowned at what she thought was a random memory popping up. She allowed herself a deep breath and settled back into her trance again.

Pat O'Brien flashed into view. Pat O'Brien, *Boys Town*. Wasn't Cagney in that, too? No, Mickey Rooney. But Pat O'Brien's image had fled, and Tam decided to go wherever this was leading, even if it appeared her mind was doing a Late, Late Movie gig instead of picking up a valid lead from the rug samples.

A new image moved into the darkness. Fighting, soldiers, guns. A momentary sound of artillery came and left; a distant war, in black and white, flashed and faded in the void. She stared again into the blankness, but a sarcastic thought escaped: *What next? John Wayne?* Despite her light trance, anger flooded through her. What did this have to do with the Gambetti boy's murder? Certainly Cagney and O'Brien hadn't done it, and there was no war in south Philadelphia. Then, the connection came: fighting, fireworks, 4th of July. Maybe she was on the right track. She concentrated twice as hard on the rug samples, thinking *Nicky Gambetti, murder.*

A face began to form in her mind, impressions rather than a visual picture. They dissipated, then Tam had the strangest sensation of falling and the feeling of surprise that came with it. The falling sensation fled and suddenly a clearly visual image broke through the darkness. She stared at the face in the second before it, too, vanished.

Tam stayed in her trance another minute, then decided to come out of it. She didn't want to lose the details of that unknown face. She slowly increased her intake of breath, which had shallowed during the trance when her body entered the sleep-like state of relaxation. In fact, her body had gone to sleep while her mind stayed conscious.

When her normal breathing returned, Tam opened her eyes and gently moved her arms and legs, both slightly numbed and heavy from the weight of the trance. Circulation restored, she stretched languidly and allowed herself a luxurious yawn. Late-night trances always did make her sleep well.

She grabbed a pen and notepaper from her bedroom desk and sat down to record the face she'd seen. She wrote of the war scene she'd witnessed, noting its symbolism of the 4th of July celebration. Did it tie into Nicky Gambetti's murder on that day? Was the killer a service man, or a veteran? Then she described the face that appeared after the war scene, recalling each detail as best she could:

'Male, Caucasian, appearing fifty-sixty years old, balding, eyes dark but color undetermined, long hook-like nose, small lips, high cheekbones, sparse eyebrows, high forehead. Face slightly narrow, eyes well-situated, neither too close nor too far

61

apart, ears average size but protruding slightly away from head. Hair has slight wave to it, a mix of light brown and dull grey. Looks intelligent but . . . '

Tam paused and rummaged for the right words.

'Looks intelligent but has detached air about him. Hard to express what I sensed. Perhaps aloof and cold personality, or perhaps an emotional withdrawal stemming from some crisis.'

Tam reread the description. Nothing was missing. She folded it up, rewrapped the rug fibers, and stuck them both into her handbag. It was nearly three a.m. She covered David where he lay on the couch quietly with his blanket. No use awakening him. It was his favorite weekend sleeping spot.

Tam moved to the bedroom, random thoughts intruding once more. Cagney, O'Brien, Asher. She wouldn't have minded Ash sharing her bed tonight. If only he'd notice her outside of their friendship and her psychic talents. Of course, she'd want more than a one-night fling. Maybe that was why he hadn't made a move since her split with Bill.

Tam suddenly smiled, realizing she'd just expressed desire for another man. Not just a desire for attention or companionship. It was a nice, tingly feeling.

She'd give him the psychic info tomorrow. No use mentioning Cagney and O'Brien. Obviously leftover images from old movies.

Obviously far off base.

She fell asleep spinning lovely and lascivious fantasies about Asher. Of how good it'd feel to have him there.

4

Sunday Evening, July 7th

Walter Buehl paced, sharply agitated, up and down the solarium tiles in his Society Hill apartment. The phone stayed silent, despite his frantic hope, his wanting it to ring. The Sunday paper lay open on the table to the Gambetti murder story. He sought to calm himself, a repetitive act since Dr. Robbins's phone call on Tuesday night. The thought of Tony's escaping, after having been safely incarcerated for over forty years, had cut into the peaceful framework of his life.

He picked up the kitchen extension, dialing the institution again. The switchboard answered this time and connected him to Dr. Robbins.

'Dr. Robbins? Walter Buehl here. Have you heard anything on Tony?'

Dr. Robbins's irritation showed in a loud unmasked sigh. It was 9:00 p.m. and he wanted home.

Tony Buehl had escaped on Tuesday, in the preparation and excitement two days before the hospital's July 4th celebration. The baker's truck had pulled up to deliver the hot dog and hamburger buns, the donuts and the cookies, outside the kitchen on the right wing of the building. And Tony, doing work therapy there, suddenly disappeared.

An extensive search of the hospital grounds culled nothing. The baker's truck revealed the usual breads and pastries. They signed the driver's packing slip and, giving him clearance, let him drive off. Later, finishing a delivery, he discovered, along with baked goods filched, the method of Tony's escape. One of the sturdy metal racks, three and one half feet each in width, height and depth, showed soft bread loaves crushed into a concave shape by the weight of some indentation. Other undamaged loaves lay scattered on the truck floor. Tony Buehl, who had never grown out of his diminutive stature since his incarceration at age eleven, had flattened the inside loaves on one of the bottom racks to fit his crouched and tightened body and arranged the remaining loaves to cover him completely in front. As the soft loaf rack sat between other racks and Tony was accustomed to keeping quiet, he escaped detection in the darkened interior of the truck. Chalk one up for Tony, the doctor thought grimly.

It should have been an easy task to find a runaway inmate carrying a fair load of unbagged bakery treats. But Tony Buehl and his stolen goods vanished.

Robbins wished Walter Buehl would vanish, too. He could imagine the bristling rigid expression on Walter Buehl's face. Everything was ordered and rigid in the man — the sharp hook nose; the small dark eyes too close to it; the tall, stiff frame; even the thinning hair styled firmly into place. Didn't he know they were doing what they could? Tony Buehl had been classified non-homicidal since 1954, ten years after the tragedy with his mother. Yet Walter Buehl, his brother, insisted he was a walking time bomb about to explode upon the unsuspecting public.

In fact, Tony Buehl might have been released into his brother's custody years ago, had Walter Buehl not blocked it vehemently. His position as an executive vice-president of the Delaware Valley Bank made him a powerful man to deal with. Outside psychiatric evaluations were ordered, Robbins's own evaluation was challenged in front of the State Board, and Tony Buehl was found mentally unfit for re-entry into the world. To hear his brother talk, you would think Walter Buehl was medically motivated and wracked with concern for the safety of all Philadelphia and its surrounding neighbors. Robbins, outnumbered, fought for a while, then was quietly told to drop his stance. Walter Buehl's sharp aversion to his brother went deliberately unnoticed and Tony remained hospitalized, seemingly inured to it.

Until now, it appeared.

Walter Buehl's rasp broke into the doctor's reverie, his voice authoritative, despite his agitation. 'Dr. Robbins, are you there?'

'Yes, Mr. Buehl, I'm here. And as I've

told you before,' he paused to let a silent *for the one-hundredth time* sink in, 'we're doing everything possible to recover your brother and return him to the hospital.' He could just about hear the sharp rush of air sucked through the tunnels of Walter Buehl's nostrils and expelled in righteous indignation.

'Time may *just* have run out, Dr. Robbins.'

'Mr. Buehl,' he started.

'Did you read the Sunday *Inquirer* today, Doctor?'

Robbins stifled his own growing anger. 'No.'

'A young boy was murdered, Dr. Robbins, by an unseen maniac.'

'What does one thing have to do with the other, Mr. Buehl? I've told you many a time, your brother is no longer homicidal.'

'Not according to other experts, Doctor — who, I might remind you, overruled you in the past.'

Dr. Robbins paused to rub his eyes beneath his glasses with his thumb and forefinger. 'Mr. Buehl, they did not rule

Tony homicidal, only *potentially* homicidal, which is a whole different barrel of apples. Any human being, if pushed to the right limit, is potentially homicidal, but social training precludes our acting on that potential in most cases. At the most, it is a minor notation on Tony's diagnosis — a *caution*, if you will, due to his childhood trauma. His overall diagnosis is not homicidal in nature; it's classified as regressive hysteria. In fact, Tony's now little more than an overgrown child who can't cope with adult standards and needs to be watched over because he may be hurt by others, rather than a maniac who hurts others. He's nearly still eleven years old in his mind and your concern should be for what might befall him, out there alone, rather than building him into some murdering aggressive in your mind. I assure you that this young boy's murder and poor Tony are entirely unconnected.'

'Your assurances mean little to me, Doctor. I know my brother far better than you, having seen his violent behavior, no matter how much you may have repressed it through drugs and therapy. It doesn't appear you take me seriously. So be it, but be advised I intend to call in other authorities to alert them to Tony's escape and its *potential danger*. Tony's a bad apple and, if you'll excuse the cold cliché, you just might find he's spoiled your barrel.'

Dr. Robbins felt his tiredness overwhelm him. An invisible weight seemed to drain his last drop of energy. He glanced at the clock. Nearly 10:00 p.m. 'So be it,' he mimicked. 'I will call you if we get any news on your brother. Good night.'

He hung up the phone, capitalizing on Walter Buehl's silence to cut off any further response. With his workload, every unnecessary minute saved was golden. And Buehl's panic, while potentially feasible, was, knowing Tony all these years, basically ludicrous.

★   ★   ★

Monday Night, July 8th

The Police Administration Building at 8th and Race Streets was called the

Roundhouse because of its design. Its two circular, four-story buildings were joined together like a figure eight. It was large and impressive but it more resembled a pair of handcuffs than a cosmic symbol of infinity.

Walter Buehl, dressed in a light gray summer suit and appearing the epitome of coolness, did not like being ignored. The air conditioning in the Roundhouse wasn't circulating fully — the air just a notch above tepid — but that was not the reason for his fidgeting about on the bench. He had been treated atrociously ever since arriving at the visitor's entrance on the ground floor, where a beefy-faced officer behind the glass partition asked him his business there. When he answered he had information on a murder, the officer rang the Homicide Division, asking him which murder. Buehl told him it was private. The officer spoke to Homicide, then directed Buehl through the double doors and around to the front desk. A detective would be down shortly to escort him up to Homicide.

It took ten minutes for the police

71

detective to arrive. They rode up to the first floor in a cantankerous elevator, which took another two minutes to arrive. Buehl began telling his story in the elevator but the detective stopped him. 'I'm not the person you'll be talking to. You'd better save it for him.' Buehl stared at him incredulously as they exited the elevator. 'Who will I be talking to?' Buehl asked the detective.

'Whoever's available next. There's two cases ahead of you, sir.' He led Buehl through the door and instructed him to sit on the vinyl-covered bench that served as a vestibule to Homicide.

It appeared the two cases before him were a purse-snatching in which the girl's fiancé was badly knifed attempting to stop it, and a druggie who had murdered another addict for his heroin. Buehl picked up snatches of conversation as he waited, eyeing a suspicious bag of white powder dumped on the desk beside the unkempt man.

Buehl shifted impatiently on the uncomfortable bench. He detested being kept waiting while they talked with human scum and unfortunate fools. He remembered Tony's vehemence, his furious ire so easily triggered all those years ago, and the horrid arguments that led to their mother's grisly murder — an unwilling memory in his mind.

He watched as the one detective led the druggie away to book him. He turned his attention to the girl, the purse snatch victim, who cried soundlessly while she answered the detective's questions. Buehl hoped she would be finished soon. Time was being wasted and his brother was at large.

★　★　★

Sergeant Dennis Colby wrapped up the paperwork on the purse-snatch attack. The fiancée, in critical condition at Hahnemann Hospital, was still unconscious. He told the girl they'd do everything possible to locate her stolen goods and apprehend the attacker. He did not tell her there was a good chance the criminal would get away clean. Her description of the man was vague and could fit a dozen people in one five-block radius and a dozen more in the next. The knifing had been unexpected and quick, the man departing in swift flight. He told her it was possible her purse might be found and returned to her, but she should report her stolen credit cards immediately. The girl, a first-time victim, appreciated any guiding strength, shook up as she was. She thanked the Sergeant and started to leave. 'Oh, Miss!' Colby called after her. She turned at the doorway. 'I hope your fiancée will be all right.'

'Thank you,' the girl said through fresh tears. He watched her smile bravely as she left.

He turned his attention to the solitary man on the bench. 'Sir?'

Walter Buehl came forward and stood by the desk. 'A sin,' he started as an opener. 'A sweet young girl like that and her boyfriend being attacked on the street.'

'Yeah,' Colby answered. 'Her fiancée shouldn't have tried to fight the man off. You can't tell if there's a hidden weapon or how desperate the attacker is. So what can I do for you, sir?'

Buehl looked at the young blond-haired detective with his Scandinavian features. He resented having to deal with an obvious underling. Once they'd heard his story, they'd escort him swiftly up the chain of command. Of that he was sure.

'I believe I have evidence of who killed that young boy.'

'What young boy, sir?'

'The teenager who was killed on the 4th of July. What was his name? Gambetti?'

Sergeant Colby's eyes widened sharply. 'Please sit down, Mr. — '

'Buehl.' He watched Colby's arm as it motioned toward the chair. This was more like it. He sat down stiffly in the hard-backed chair. Colby readied his pen and notepad.

'My name is Sergeant Colby. Please go on, Mr. Buehl.'

'Well . . . isn't there someone higher? An investigative unit I should be talking to?'

Dennis Colby nearly blanched at the

innuendo but kept a straight face. 'Detectives process the incoming data. Normally, Mr. Buehl, I wouldn't be doing this interview but we're short-handed today. What have you got to tell us?' He wondered if this guy was a nut, publicity-seeker, then decided against it from the look of him.

'Very well. I have reason to believe my brother may have murdered this young man.'

'And what makes you think that?' He was impressed by the coldness in Buehl's voice. Definitely not a family type. Definitely had no love for his brother.

'My brother was incarcerated in the State sanatorium up to last Tuesday.'

'Was?'

'Yes. He escaped and there's been no trace of him since. He's somewhere at large in the city. He couldn't have gotten far. He had no money.'

'You don't sound concerned for him.'

'My brother was incarcerated for murder, Sergeant.'

Colby got interested. 'Criminally insane.'

'That's right.'

76

'Okay, we'll definitely check your lead. But what makes you think he murdered Nicky Gambetti?'

'He's murdered before. He's got a violent temper. I've been witness to it.'

'Okay, let's get some facts. I want his name, age, description. Which state institution he's a patient with and who his attending physician is.'

Walter Buehl duly offered the information. Colby scribbled it down on his notepad. 'When was your brother Tony first incarcerated, Mr. Buehl?'

'In 1944.'

Colby looked up sharply then lowered his eyes to the pad. 'And what was the crime?'

The corners of Buehl's mouth twitched as Colby looked up at him again. 'He murdered our mother.' When Colby didn't respond quickly enough, he reiterated, 'He stabbed her to death with a kitchen knife.' Colby noted that Buehl's eyes seemed to film over with a blankness and his skin turned pasty white at the memory of the method.

'That must have been traumatic for

you, Mr. Buehl.' He wrote the information down while talking. 'Do you mind
my asking how old you and your brother
were when this happened?'

'I was eight,' Walter Buehl answered, as
if the memory was seared into his brain,
'and I believe Tony was, yes, eleven.'

Now Colby looked directly up at him.
'This sounds like a family tragedy, Mr.
Buehl. It may not be connected at all with
the Gambetti case.'

'My brother is diagnosed homicidal,
Sergeant, and he has escaped from his
protective environment.' His glare made
Colby feel hotter.

'We will check it out, Mr. Buehl. I'd
like to get some information on you, your
residence and work address, so we can
contact you if we need to.'

Buehl again obliged him. Finishing, he
added, 'You will put out an APB on Tony,
won't you?'

Dennis Colby smiled at the jargon.
'We'd like to talk to this Dr. Robbins first.
If he took off from Byberry, we probably
have a radio message out on him already.'

The crow feet at the corner of Buehl's

eyes wrinkled deeply. 'He's dangerous, Sergeant Colby. You've got to find him.'

'I understand your concern, Mr. Buehl, and we'll get on it right away. But don't get all worked up over the Gambetti case. It may have been an unrelated incident. But we'll definitely check it out.'

'I'm convinced it *is* related!'

Colby permitted himself the tiniest of laughs at the ultra-seriousness on Walter Buehl's face. 'Well, we will check it out, Mr. Buehl. And we'll get back to you as soon as we have something definite to report.'

'You don't want me to wait until you check it out?'

'No, that's not necessary. It might take a day or two.'

'A day or two. Someone else could be murdered by then!'

Colby sighed. The man was becoming a pain. 'Mr. Buehl, I know you're upset, but trust me. We'll get back to you as quickly as possible. Don't let your imagination get the better of you. As I've said, your brother may not be connected to any murder.' He tried to sound cheerful.

But Walter Buehl remained stone-faced. 'And who will be calling me back?'

'Either me or Lieutenant Lowenstein in the squad handling the Gambetti case. Probably me.' He said the last deliberately; although it was true, it made the egotistical Buehl squirm and made Colby feel vindicated from the earlier caste system sneer.

Buehl rose from his chair majestically. 'I expect some action, Sergeant.'

'Yes, sir. We'll be back in touch soon.' He stood as well to signal the interview's end. But Buehl wasn't quite done, his gaze fixed on Colby.

'And Sergeant Colby . . . ' He spoke like a four-star general addressing a private.

'Yes?'

'That Dr. Robbins. Typical institution doctor. Doesn't want to admit the seriousness of the situation. That Lieutenant Lorenstein?'

'Lowenstein.'

'He may have to go beyond Robbins to discover the full nature of Tony's condition and the dangers therein. He may want to check with the State Board. Their findings are more conclusive.'

'I'll make a note of that.'

When Buehl didn't move, he wrote 'State Board' down on the pad.

Buehl appeared satisfied. Colby wondered if he should salute, but Walter Buehl solved the problem by nodding and letting himself out of the tangle of desks and police personnel without a further word.

★　★　★

Wednesday, July 10th, 11:00 a.m.

Asher put down the medical report on Tony Buehl which Dr. Robbins had sent him. The frown creasing his jaw was caused by the current photo supplied with the profile and the small notepaper he now picked up in his hand. Tam's clear description of the man she'd envisioned glared at him. It, curiously, fitted Tony Buehl. Yet according to the doctor, Anthony Michael Buehl was harmless.

Ash checked the present diagnosis again. Regressive hysteria. And reread the personal letter that Dr. Robbins had sent to the Department along with the file.

Tony is nothing more than an aged child, it read. *The Philadelphia Police Department, in its efforts to find him, as a missing person requiring hospitalization, should keep this strongly in mind. If located and apprehended by one of your officers, he may react in a frightened and shy manner. The mention of my name will have a calming effect. If the officer then obtains his trust, he may respond in a juvenile manner, looking for reassurance that he is being taken 'home,' showing excitement on being driven in a police vehicle. Television has shaped a large part of his viewpoint of the outside world. He may relate your officers to characters in police dramas.*

All of the above may occur in the event of Tony's apprehension, but no dangerous implications are projected. Tony's one brush with homicide was, for all his brother's invective, a case of temporary insanity due to an unstable home life situation caused by wartime circum-stances. His act was self-negating; in essence, he became emotionally crippled by it; hence, his regressive hysteria.

If you need any further information, please feel free to contact me. Under all circumstances, I appreciate the Police Department's help in attempting to locate Tony Buehl.

Sincerely,

Alexander Robbins, M.D.

Ash put the letter down and dialed the number at the head of the hospital's stationery. The similarity between Tony Buehl and Tam's description spooked him. He wanted to be certain Robbins's calm diagnosis was correct before phoning Walter Buehl with his findings.

He dialed the number almost reluctantly. He felt somewhat guilty questioning a psychiatrist's diagnosis based on a psychic's description. But not all things were rational that were real. Including murder. And murder was on his mind.

The operator at the state sanatorium put him through to Robbins.

'Lieutenant Lowenstein. How are you?'

'Fine, Doctor. I've read your letter to the Department concerning Tony Buehl. There's just one thing I've got to know. How potentially homicidal could he be?'

Alex Robbins answered in a soft quiet drawl. 'No more than the average man in the street. In fact, less. Tony's regressive hysteria makes him dependent, timid in a threatening situation. He'd run rather than fight; and if he had to fight, he'd probably do it ineffectively, no matter what the method. But one thing bothers me. What causes you to doubt my report, with Tony being under my care for innumerable years? Has his brother Walter convinced you otherwise?'

Asher caught his breath and hedged. 'No, that's not it. Sergeant Colby's already filled me in on Walter Buehl's impassioned hatred toward his brother.'

'Then what?'

Ash sighed; he knew it was audible. Robbins seemed to wait patiently. 'Look, doc. You may find this a little unconventional. We have a psychic working on the Gambetti case. She's good and I know her personally. She's not a wacko case. If

84

anything, she's reluctant about her ability. She meditated over some blood-stained strands of rug from the Gambetti homicide and came up with a very definite description of an older man. A description which fits the photo you sent of Tony Buehl.' He waited for something, he wasn't sure what: a touch of humored incredulity, a condescending but curt response. It didn't matter. He had to play the scene out, even to a dead end.

'Psychometry,' Dr. Robbins said.

'Excuse me?'

'That's what you're describing, Lieutenant. Psychometry. From a psychic description, it's the act of picking up paranormal information from an inanimate object. And you say this psychic has been accurate?'

'More than she wants to admit.'

There was a pause on Robbins's line. Thinking perhaps. Then an intake of breath. 'I don't want to put the lady down, but I'd say she's wrong about Tony.'

'That's what I needed to hear.'

'Sorry if I've disappointed you.'

'You haven't.' Ash fingered the photograph of Tony Buehl. 'To tell you the truth, although the basic description fits, I couldn't quite picture this guy as a murderer. Not at this stage of his life. You know, Dr. Robbins, our divisional detectives are actually responsible for missing persons, not Homicide, unless some murder is involved. Do you have any idea where he might be staying? That I might pass on to the Northeast Detective Division?'

'Not at his brother's. That's for certain. He and Walter have a cool relationship, to put it bluntly, and that mostly on Walter's part. He's done immeasurable damage by keeping him incarcerated, although living with Walter would do even greater damage, I'm sure.'

'Keeping him incarcerated?'

'It's a long story, Lieutenant Lowenstein. Let's just say there are powers greater than mine that dance to a vastly different drum.'

'And so Tony made a break for freedom because little brother finagled and wouldn't let him out.'

'Close. I think that's the root. He may have felt he was playing a game, at least initially. I'd really like to know where he's staying, that he's all right. His child's frame of mind would have had him seeking help by now, telling people he was lost or bad, if he were still homeless and hungry.'

'You think he's found shelter?'

'You may find this odd but he's a winsome personality. No traces of the aggression that led to his mother's death.'

'I'll pass that along to the Northeast Division.'

'Thank you. So I've convinced you it wasn't Tony?'

Asher considered it. 'Yes. But unfortunately, it doesn't answer my major question.'

'Who killed the Gambetti boy.'

'Yeah. Look, thanks, doc, for all your help. I guess I'll go back to square one now.'

'If I can help you in any way, please don't hesitate to give me a call.'

'Thank you . . . have a good day.'

Cripes, Asher thought as he heard Dr.

Robbins's respondent goodbye and hung up the phone. Even shrinks could sound departmental. If he needed Robbins's help, he wouldn't worry about hesitating. But it was nice of the man to offer. And he seemed to know a lot about this parapsychology business. He wondered if Robbins would talk to Tam. He might help her iron out her fears about using her strange talent. Nothing in life was easy, he thought, whether gumshoe or mystic. The facts were hard to find and, once found, sometimes hard to deal with.

As he dialed Walter Buehl's number to tell him Tony was off the hook, he couldn't know how hard one man would find it to deal with *that* fact.

Walter Buehl only dealt with things one way.

His way.

5

Thursday, July 11th

Asher Lowenstein fingered the styrofoam cup filled with coffee, clutched it and raised it to his lips. He anticipated the warm sweet rush it would make trickling down his throat. At thirty-five years old and married to a job with minimal pleasures, his coffee was his morning companion and first pleasure of the day.

He had awakened at the usual hour in his apartment off Oxford Avenue in the Northeast to find he was out of coffee and had forgotten his intention to buy more the night before. Grumbling, he had dressed and driven downtown to the Roundhouse. On the way in he stopped by a coffee shop, carrying out a large, capable of opening each eye completely and then some.

The tangy liquid hit his taste buds and throat just as Colby's phone squealed out a sharp ring. Colby, who had complacently been shuffling paperwork when Ash came in, told him Walter Buehl had arrived downstairs and was asking to see him. He said this with a laughing smirk Asher didn't appreciate. Buehl. It had taken him long enough to get off the phone with that irritating man yesterday without resorting to foul language. Ash looked at his watch moodily. 9:15 a.m. Cripes. He sent Colby to escort Buehl up to Homicide, then pulled an extra hard-backed chair sitting helter-skelter beside the next desk over to the right of his own. He sat down again and took a long draught of his coffee, steeling himself. *Damn*, he thought, *and first thing in the morning.*

As Colby opened the door to Homicide, Buehl brushed past him. He seemed to scrutinize the other unoccupied desks, the unadorned quiet atmosphere. Asher stood up and motioned to the extra chair. 'I'm Asher Lowenstein, Mr. Buehl. Would you care to have a seat?'

But Walter Buehl continued to eye the nearly empty room, as Colby returned to his desk and resumed his work. 'They're either on vacation or out on cases,' Asher answered his open stare.

Buehl began his diatribe on his way over to the chair Asher offered him. 'You gents do have a problem keeping law and order.'

Asher waited until he had seated himself, then asked, 'What can I do for you, Mr. Buehl?'

Walter Buehl sat ramrod straight, his back never touching the back of the chair. 'Mr. Lowenstein,' he eyed the nameplate on the desk, 'you can begin by taking me seriously.'

For no other reason than to keep the ranks straight, Asher corrected him. 'It's Lieutenant Lowenstein. And I have taken you seriously, Mr. Buehl. We've checked out the facts and your brother isn't a suspect.'

'A foolish assumption. To begin with, my brother is on the loose and he's dangerous. I live in fear that he'll come for me or hurt another innocent victim any day now.'

'According to Dr. Robbins, Tony is now

harmless, Mr. Buehl. The Philadelphia Police Department sees no viable reason to consider him a suspect in the Gambetti case. However, we do have a general radio message out on him to find him and return him to the state hospital.' A tinge of distaste hit his last words despite his attempt to keep his voice modulated and calm. 'We're following up new leads on the Gambetti case.'

'You have another suspect?'

'No, not yet.'

'Just as I thought,' Buehl said fervently. Asher had a sense of deja vu staring at him and realized he bore a close resemblance to his older brother. But the warm gentle personality ascribed to Tony Buehl was missing in his brother. Walter Buehl wore his own unique cold and twisted marks upon his face. The resemblance ended with the flesh.

'Mr. — *Lieutenant* Lowenstein, you're asking for serious trouble if you don't conduct an all-out search for him for what he is: a killer. Another murder may occur and the public will not be kind.' Buehl's voice rose by decibels; his volume, Asher was sure, filtering into the hall outside.

'Mr. Buehl, I'm sorry to have to dispute you, but your brother's involvement in this case is closed. Our Northeast Detective Division is now handling his status as a missing person due to his mental age. If you want, I can give you their phone number, although Dr. Robbins has given us all the information we need concerning finding Tony and I've relayed it to them.'

'Dr. Robbins!' Walter Buehl spat it out and Ash noticed a muscle in his neck twitch momentarily. 'The man is a quack, doesn't know the first think about real homicidal behavior.' He was beginning to irritate, his voice still notching upward. 'He's a product of a system. They *drug* him there and call him cured.'

'Drug who?'

'Tony!' As the last was shouted, the door to the captain's office at the center of the room opened simultaneously. Frank Anunzio leaned his head and shoulders out, his trim bulk resting against the door. His eyes locked with

Asher's. 'Is this room becoming reserved for primal therapy?' he asked cautiously. 'Is everything all right out here?' He inched further past the doorway to see the other occupant, back turned to him, who shifted slightly at the sound of Anunzio's voice.

Asher started to reply, but never got the chance.

'Walt?' The captain swung the door open and stepped out. 'Walt Buehl!'

Walter Buehl was suddenly on his feet. 'Frank! What the hell! Am I glad to see you! Is this your stomping grounds?'

Ash watched Buehl's entire mannerism change, slip into suave Center City business profile. Captain Anunzio slapped Buehl on the back. 'Yep. But what brings you here?'

'I believe I have information on a case you're handling that could be highly pertinent.'

Asher felt his tenuous hope of pushing Walter Buehl out of his life slip away. Walter Buehl indicted him with the sweep of his hand. 'I'm afraid Lieutenant Lowenstein doesn't understand the gravity involved.'

The low-key authority of the man's voice was unquestionable. Ash said nothing, choosing to wait for Anunzio's cue. He shot Anunzio a glance: *You play the next card. I've played my hand already.*

Anunzio read him right. 'Walter, why don't you come back to my office and fill me in on this privately. Lieutenant Lowenstein, I'm sure, has done everything necessary so far on his end. If you give me another lead on whatever matter you've come here on, I assure you we'll leap right on it and explore it to exhaustion.'

Buehl was silent. He reminded Ash of an animal sniffing out a new direction to proceed in, wavering uncertainly at a new set of scents on a path. He wondered if Buehl would repeat his spiel in front of him to undermine his authority in front of the Captain. But the wavering made him bet Buehl wouldn't. He'd continue to conduct his power play more privately in Anunzio's office, carefully downplaying his familial paranoia.

'I expect a personal conversation would be best,' Buehl conceded with the air of a man who's been unfairly wounded. 'It does concern my family, but I do hope, after I've explained, you'll impress the lieutenant with the need for media coverage.'

The words 'media coverage' raised Frank Anunzio's eyebrows. He looked at Asher.

'It concerns the Gambetti case and Mr. Buehl's missing brother,' Asher offered. 'You're my superior. If you request further action on Anthony Buehl, I'll implement it.' He was tired; his coffee was probably cold.

Anunzio's brows creased. The Gambetti case was hot and Ash knew he was feeling the pressure of the press. The very word 'media' could spell pariah.

'Come on.' Captain Anunzio gestured to Walter Buehl. 'Let's talk.' Buehl followed him to his office with a cursory nod to Asher. The door to Anunzio's office shut.

Sergeant Colby, who had stayed steadfastly silent during the whole exchange, turned a cynical smile toward Asher. 'Well? Did you survive him?'

'Barely,' he grumbled. 'I'm glad Anunzio rescued me.'

He looked sourly at the dregs in his styrofoam cup. 'Feel like getting us some coffee?'

* * *

'He does resemble the man I visualized.' Tam looked down at the photo Ash had given her. 'But I'll tell you something else . . . he's not the man.'

'You get the same feeling?' Asher asked, sipping the fresh cup of coffee Colby had finally gotten for him.

'You're not supposed to trust a photograph,' Tam said, explaining her art. 'Photos can be doctored, touched up to disguise the true person. But they usually can't change the eyes themselves — and the eyes are, as they say, the mirrors to the soul. These are not the eyes of a murderer; they're the eyes of a gentle, hurt person.' She handed the photo back to him. 'Tony Buehl's not your man. But you were right on the resemblance. I can see why it shook you.'

Ash let out a sigh of exasperation. The lab hadn't come up with anything new. They were at a dead end. 'Have *you* come up with anything new?' he now asked Tam, his only other option.

Tam was thoughtful before replying. 'Well, I guess there are two things I could mention. The first was something I picked up during the meditation, but I felt — I still feel — it was probably a fluke. I kept seeing film clips from old war movies and two vintage actors: James Cagney and Pat O'Brien. At first I thought the killer might be a vet, but it seemed too much like a random, unconnected thought.'

'Tam,' Asher chided her gently, 'you've got to learn to give me *everything* you get, no matter how ridiculous or out of bounds it seems. You told me yourself that real psychic data sometimes comes in symbols that don't seem to relate to what you're searching for, but which prove very much on the mark in the end. Now that bit about war could mean a vet who's still emotionally disturbed. The guys who made it back from the jungles in Vietnam are still carrying a lot of psychological weight. I can check out any vets in the area that have a history of mental problems or arrests.'

Tam smiled, her dimples making her look buoyant. 'I'll remember to tell you everything from now on. But you have to admit, the bit about Cagney and O'Brien and World War II was irrelevant.'

Ash looked up abruptly from the pad he'd been writing on. 'World War II? Maybe not.' His face looked troubled. 'Tony Buehl's father was killed in World War II. It led to Tony's instability as a youth and culminated in his frenzied argument with his mother. Which ended in her death at his hand.'

'Ash,' Tam reminded him, 'his father died in World War II. Not Tony or his mother. It's a long shot, an extremely long one. At any rate, I still say Tony Buehl's not the killer.'

'Well, at least you've given me another lead. A potential one.' His pencil was circling the word 'vet' on the pad.

He was glad Tam had dropped in to see him. The morning interview with Walter Buehl had irked him badly, souring his mood until Tam's arrival lightened it. 'Look. It's past one o'clock. Care for some lunch, lady?'

'Sounds great.' She rose, shouldering her handbag.

Frank Anunzio emerged from his office. He saw Tam and brightened. 'Well, how are you, my dear?'

'I'm fine, thank you, Captain.'

'Do you mind if I have a few words with Asher?'

'No. I'll leave if you want me to.'

'No, no. Stay. It'll only take a minute.' He turned to Asher, who rose from his desk. 'I've handled Walter Buehl. He's obviously distressed over his brother's disappearance. I also called Dr. Robbins, who pretty much told me what he told you. I excused myself a few minutes to make that call out of Walter's earshot. He seems to have an emotional dislike towards that man, but Robbins is Tony Buehl's attending physician. I told Walter that media coverage right now might hamper our search for Tony, causing him to run farther, or cause another murder, if the killer's on an ego trip. He seemed to calm down and listen.'

'Do you think Tony Buehl's the murderer?'

'No. I've read your report, Lieutenant Lowenstein, and Dr. Robbins's input. But Walter Buehl's an influential man in the banking community and right now he's rather upset.'

'So you fudged your words to suit him and he backed down and decided to let the police run their own department.'

Anunzio laughed. 'He didn't exactly relinquish command to me. He seemed content to let it go if I got our people in the Northeast to speed up their search for Tony. Very concerned over his brother 'killing another person.' Said if that happened we'd have to go on the airwaves with Tony's description. Look, Asher, he's a little paranoid with his brother on the loose, but if our killer keeps this a one-time homicide, I think I can keep Walter Buehl quiet.'

'Our *real* killer. I only hope he does.'

'Maybe he'll oblige us. But in the meantime, I want you to handle this case personally. For now. And how about you,

Tam? Have you come up with some new leads?'

'I was just telling Ash, Captain. I had some visuals on a war situation. The man may be a vet. And something I haven't mentioned to Asher yet.'

'May I stay and hear?' the captain asked politely.

'Sure. Asher, this may seem like a prejudgment, but you told me to mention it all.'

'Speak,' Asher commanded.

'Well, that picture of that man I visualized keeps popping up in my mind. And with it, an attitude. His attitude. He hates teenagers. Has some sort of personal vendetta against them. A murderous hateful vendetta.'

'Then it's an emotional motive. That's what you're telling me you're picking up.'

'Purely,' Tam said firmly.

Asher and the Captain eyed each other. 'Let's hope he got his anger out with the first one,' the captain said dryly.

★ ★ ★

Saturday, July 13th

'Are you sure it's safe?' Annie asked as they rumbled over a still-cobblestoned section of Rising Sun Avenue. 'I mean, this isn't too far from Byberry.'

Santa Ana had heard, through a compatriot in the Northeast, of a classical guitar priced very compatibly within the household budget. 'Listen, Annie, they don't have cops standin' every thirty yards lookin' for runaways. And I doubt if they have a wanted poster in the music store.' He parked the car two blocks from Cottman Avenue and proceeded to move his bulk from the car. Annie, Murphy and Claire followed suit, and Scrugs nudged Tony to come on. But Tony sat rooted.

'I don't wanna go out. I'm afraid they're gonna catch me.'

Santa looked about to chide Annie for her earlier comment, then stopped. Putting each other down wasn't their way. Live and let live. 'Stay with him?' he half-asked Scrugs. Scrugs grunted compliance. He settled back into the car with Tony as the others trooped across the street to the tiny music store down the block.

He and Tony stared across the street, then Scrugs eyed the neighborhood tavern directly to the right of his opened car window. Rivulets of sweat glistened on his arm, elbow against the silver rim. 'Listen, Tony, stay in the car. I'm gonna get a quart of beer.'

Tony stayed silent, and Scrugs expected him to protest, but then he said, 'Okay.'

Scrugs opened the car door, admonishing like a father to a son, 'Stay here. If you leave, I'll bust your ass in.'

Tony merely nodded.

Scrugs slammed the door and went into the tavern. It was crowded, 3:00 p.m. on a Saturday afternoon, the local trade well-plied in the air-conditioned belly-up-to-the-bar atmosphere. A large screen at one end showed some cable sports and the barmaid scurried back and forth behind the counter, serving customers. Scrugs waited ten minutes before she caught him between two seated barflies, caught his raised hand gesture over the heads of the seated men, and asked,

'What can I get for ya?'

'A quart of Bud,' Scrugs told her.

She scurried back to the refrigerated compartment to her right and just as quickly bagged his order. 'That'll be a buck sixty-five.'

Scrugs paid her, grabbed the bag and threaded his way through the crowd to the front door of the tavern. A jukebox, suddenly blasting country fare, drowned out the cable show as he exited.

Back in the car, with Tony still quiet — probably apprehensive over Annie's stupid worried remark — Scrugs took a couple of gulps of beer. The brew slid down, smooth and cooling. A few minutes later, Santa Ana and the rest of the crew returned. Santa gently put his new guitar in the trunk of the car. He wasn't, as he was quick to admit, an expert musician, but he could play fairly well. The others enjoyed listening and looked forward to hearing Santa's new instrument.

Scrugs shared a slug or two of his quart with the others, Tony abstaining, and they gunned the motor to leave.

'Ya see?' Santa said as they sped back

to the boulevard and home. 'Tony had nothing to worry about.'

Tony smiled, snug and safe in their protective grasp.

★ ★ ★

Walter Buehl sat uncomfortably on the barstool. The cable sports show blared to his unheeding ears. The jukebox had stopped crying its country lament, and no one had put another quarter in. Buehl sipped his Heineken and turned to his client on his right. He was only in this neighborhood watering hole because of this man, a prosperous construction owner who had built his business up from ground level to a million-dollar wealth.

The man, Michael Terrezano, had dropped the business part of the conversation: the financing of a vast retirement community in the Somerton section of the Northeast. He was now on the subject of his son, a twenty-two-year-old college dropout who refused to enter his father's business. 'I tell him, 'Andy, you got it made. I'll set you up. You'll learn the

106

business. When I retire, you got a going concern.' What does he say? 'But, Pop, I don't know if I want construction.''

Buehl took a gulp of beer. 'No appreciation.' He became aware of a short, scruffy-looking man wavering behind him and Michael, his hair long and appearing greasy, his forehead beaded with droplets of sweat. Buehl registered immediate distaste and took another swig of beer. The barmaid behind the counter came over, positioned herself between Walter and his client, and addressed the scruffy interloper. 'What can I get for ya?'

'A quart of Bud.'

Buehl watched silently as she scurried back to the refrigerated compartment and just as quickly bagged the little man's order. 'That'll be a buck sixty-five,' she told him. He paid her, grabbed his bag and left. The jukebox, someone having fed it its prerequisite allotment, blared forth a new county tune, drowning out the cable again. None of the barflies seemed to mind.

'You see what I mean?' Buehl resumed

his conversation with his client. 'Take that punk that just left. I'll bet his ambition level is nil, nada, nothing. Probably never worked an honest job in his life that he didn't quit the next day.'

'Ah,' Michael said, 'you can't expect everybody to be successful. Some guys can't make it.'

'In my book, some guys can't take it. Either you've got it and use it or you're lazy and you don't. Me, I'd tell your son, 'Andy, you're coming to work in the business and you're gonna learn it whether you like it or not, cause that's what keeps the wolf from the door.''

Despite the air conditioning, the beer was making him feel hazy. He'd had the damnedest time finding a parking space earlier. The tavern, obviously a popular spot, had a full-up parking lot and that block of Rising Sun Avenue had no parking spaces large enough for his Cadillac. Luckily he had noticed an apartment complex behind the tavern, separated only by a metal fence with an open gate for residents to pass through to the tavern. He had gone around the block and parked in the apartment buildings' lot. As small an inconvenience as it seemed, it had tired him. He wouldn't have even been in this blue-collar wooden-box watering ground, a four-by-four with just enough space for the amenities, the booze, the bar and the customers, if Terrezano hadn't been an important client for the bank. But the man's riches were pulled from the bootstrap up and Terrezano was still a blue-collar at heart. Not the kind of drinking partner he was used to. But business was business.

Terrezano considered Buehl's advice on father/son relationships with the jaundiced eye of someone having tried that route and failed. 'I been through that with Andy, pulling rank and all, but it only works for a while. Then he's off, missing days, doing what he wants.'

Buehl scowled. 'Then he's no good and you should kick him out of the house and let him see what it's like on the street with an empty pocket.'

Terrezano side-glanced him. His eyebrow raised minutely. Buehl saw the subtle stiffening and realized he'd just made a serious error in judgment. He quickly revised his words. 'I mean, he's your son and you know him much better than I do, but they do say if children are forced to live on their own, they learn very quickly what life's all about.'

The man listened, shrugged noncommittally, and took a slug of his beer. 'Maybe you're right. We never tried kickin' him out.'

'That's just advice, Mike,' Buehl was quick to put in. 'You'll have to decide what's right for you. But the kid might straighten out. He's young.' He smiled.

Terrezano's pudgy affable face smiled back at the hopeful rejoinder. He smacked his lips. 'Yeah.' He looked at his watch. 'Well, I got to get goin', Walter. I think the financing looks good on the retirement housing. How's about you call me when the papers are ready to be signed?'

'Sounds good,' Buehl agreed. 'I really have to take off, too.'

Terrezano scooped up his change from the counter and sorted out a tip from it.

Buehl rose to go also. They shook hands. 'I'll call you this week,' Buehl told him.

They separated, Buehl heading out the back door and past the open gate to the residential parking lot. But as he unlocked the car door, his hand froze. Loud screaming voices suddenly hit the balmy air.

★   ★   ★

The small crowd dithered to and fro, as crowds are wont to do when unexpected tragedy strikes. Paul Mandel struggled to get to his feet but blood spurted freshly from the wound in his side. He moaned weakly from pain and fell back, lying once again on the gravel of the driveway. Someone ran for the nurse who lived in Apartment 216; another ran to phone for an ambulance. But an off-duty police-man, Joe Crissman, who lived in the middle building and had discovered Paul lying in shock on the ground, had already called for a rescue unit. 'Who did this to you, Paul?' Crissman asked him. He knew a gunshot wound when he saw one.

Paul Mandel's dark brown hair was flat with sweat; his dark eyes were glossy with fear and tears. His shock was apparently worsening. 'No good. No good. No good,' he gasped in spasmodic heaves.

'Ssh, lie still, Paul,' Crissman soothed him. 'Help is on the way.' Where the hell was rescue?

A woman's voice shrieked through the air. 'Paul!'

The boy appeared to stiffen with more pain with recognition of that agonized scream. 'Mommy,' he murmured, regressing beyond his teenage years in his torment. 'Mommy . . . '

His mother, Sophie Mandel, took one look at her son's blood and her hand flew instinctively, self-protectively, to cover her mouth.

'Get her out of here,' Crissman shouted, expecting a scene, perhaps her jostling the boy, attempting to hold him in maternal frenzy. He could explain — apologize — later. Paul was losing too much blood.

He needn't have worried. The mother was in too much of a frenzy. A gagging cough overtook her and she allowed herself to be led a short distance away. 'We have to call an ambulance,' Crissman heard her say in a sharp strangled voice.

'We already have,' someone told her, the voice velvet with sympathy. Ah, Sophie, Crissman thought, why did it have to happen to you? He felt for Paul's pulse; it was growing weaker.

A new runner came to tell him the nurse was not at home. But at that moment a siren sounded, a distant bellowing monster that increased in shrill volume as the rescue unit pulled into the apartment complex parking lot. The attendants jumped down, started emergency aid to stanch the bleeding, and removed Paul to the unit. Crissman showed his I.D. and identified the mother. He helped Sophie Mandel climb in the back of the unit, climbing in afterwards himself, helping her sit and holding her tightly.

Now Sophie Mandel was in shock and Paul Mandel was unconscious.

But, the ambulance attendant told Crissman and Sophie, he was still alive.

6

Asher Lowenstein had responded quickly to the call from Captain Katz of the Second District in Northeast Philadelphia. A police composite using Tam's description had been circulated throughout the district stations along with a bulletin on the Gambetti murder. Katz had considered the attacks too similar not to run it by Headquarters. Frank Anunzio had agreed and Asher had rushed to Jeanes Hospital, where Paul Mandel was fighting for his life.

Tam, in response to Asher's quick phone call, met him there, in case he had need of her. Sophie Mandel had already been questioned by Detective Ed Cyzwinski of the Northeast Detectives. Asher knew she was maintaining a shaky brave decorum as he introduced himself and Tam.

Sophie Mandel's face bore the stained, salty excess of dried tears. She looked and probably felt numb. Asher tried to gently draw her from her lethargy as nurses, doctors and orderlies bustled in and out of the hospital corridors beyond the waiting area. 'We know you're in a state of shock but we really need to know what happened. Perhaps it'll even help to talk.' Tam hovered nearby but her attention seemed drawn to the trauma unit down the hall where Paul Mandel lay, unresponsive.

Sophie Mandel was an educated, self-sufficient woman. Cyzwinski had filled him in on her. She had supported herself and Paul for over ten years and she wasn't prone to scenes or loss of control. But she was flesh and blood and she glanced uncertainly at Asher, as if weighing the benefit of talking against the distress it might cause. Finally she asked, 'What do you want to know?'

'The events prior to the shooting.'

Her face fell at the mention of the attack on Paul. 'Well, I didn't know of it until my neighbor knocked.' She paused, giving a bitter laugh. 'Pounded on the door. I thought the place was on fire or something. Then I ran out to the parking lot and saw.' She lapsed into silence.

'Was Paul out all afternoon? Coming home?'

'No. He was home. He had left a few minutes prior to this . . . shooting.'

'Where was he going?'

'To a carnival. He said there was a carnival somewhere. Rides and such. He just said, 'I'm going to the carnival, Mom'.'

'Did he mention anything else before he left? People he was going to meet? Anything?'

Mrs. Mandel hesitated. Then, with a faint voice as if she spoke from a distance, she said, 'No.' She sat as if weighted in the vinyl-covered chair.

Tam walked slowly over to Sophie Mandel and stood in front of her. 'You had a fight,' she said with clear but emotionless conviction.

Sophie Mandel looked up at Tam, appraising her, surprised but not shocked. The look was respectful. Mrs. Mandel had sleek blonde hair and resembled a slightly heavier Grace Kelly with her stature and fine facial features. She wasn't unglued by Tam's sudden firm remark. She inclined her head in a nod to Tam. A weak smile haunted her lips and fled. 'Yes, you're right . . . we did.'

'I'm sorry. That's all I picked up.'

'You're very good,' Sophie Mandel complimented her. Then her face appeared etherized once more. Her voice became distant again. 'The fight.'

'Could you tell us about the fight, Mrs. Mandel?' Asher murmured.

Sophie Mandel stared straight ahead, her vision riveted on the nursing station, as if such concentration would resurface the memory with minimal pain. 'Paul wanted to go to the carnival. I didn't want him to go.'

'Why not?' Asher prompted.

'Because he was grounded. He flunked two subjects last year and was going to summer school for one. His punishment was no allowance and no good times for two months. And this weekend, he rebelled.'

'Just walked out?'

'No. Paul does *not* just walk out. I did

have to try to enforce my discipline rules. Paul blew up, something he doesn't do often.' She paused, remembering. 'This time it was impossible. There was, yes, I believe it was a girl he hoped to run into at the carnival. He had met her at summer school and she'd said she might be there.'

'How badly did he blow up?'

Mrs. Mandel drew her breath in. 'Lieutenant Lowenstein, is this really necessary?'

'Yes,' Asher said simply.

Again, the quiet hesitation, and almost regal reluctance. 'He blew up badly. Cursing at me in a way Paul knows I don't approve of — not me, not anyone. It was brief but loud and I'm afraid I raised my voice, too, before I realized the windows were wide open and we could be heard.'

'By your neighbors?'

'Probably around the bend of the middle building.'

'That loud?'

'That loudly. Then, of course, I went to shut the windows and turn the air conditioning on. I'd been airing out the apartment. But before I reached one window, Paul shouted he was leaving. And before I blinked, the door slammed behind him. That's hardly ever happened.' Her voice cracked on the last sentence; she looked about to cry. Tam stood close. Ash could almost feel her trying to lend emotional support to this woman.

'And did you rush after him?'

The woman took in another breath and appeared to steady herself. 'No, I told you the neighbor alerted me to Paul's . . . shooting. I was far too upset by his behavior to do any good by confronting him further. Paul and I have a rule. When we get that upset, we separate to cool down enough to talk, usually before it escalates to the level it did to today. That's what I thought he'd do. Go outside, calm down and come in to apologize and talk.' Suddenly all the breaths she'd taken in came out in a large spent sigh.

'Thank you for telling us that,' Asher said.

'Did it help?'

'I think it did.'

'I don't see how.'

'It helped me to get a possible M.O. on the attacker. Some identification.'

'I still don't understand.'

'I'll explain further when I'm sure. Mrs. Mandel, do you think Tam could go in to observe Paul?'

'I'll check with the doctor.' She got up to ask.

When she was out of earshot, Asher murmured, 'I think your man hasn't finished his vendetta.'

Tam nodded glumly. 'If this is connected,' she added.

*　*　*

The cool, antiseptic hospital room and the unconscious boy on the bed seemed to unglue Tam. Again, the earlier dream, one month ago, of David's murder came back clearly and forcibly to her. She thought quickly of her sympathy for, and her desire to help, Paul Mandel and, correspondingly, his stoic mother.

Sophie Mandel stood beside her. 'Can you do that psychic healing stuff?' She gazed at Tam with eyes that pleaded yet were hollow with maternal fear.

Tam answered the gaze. She could feel the woman's pain. 'Yes. You can do it, too. Here.' She cupped her hand lightly around Paul's limp one. 'Go around to the other side and hold his other hand loosely, just so your palm and fingers touch it. That's fine. Now it's most important that you believe. Believe you can call him out of this coma. Call to him mentally and tell him you love him and want him to revive. And while you do this, imagine that you have pure, sparkling white energy coursing through you and it flows out, through your hand, in a white light that will envelop Paul. Imagine this light healing him.'

'Imagine?'

'Imagine you see and feel it. We all have energy transmitting outward from ourselves every day, affecting ourselves and other people. You can control this energy. But you have to visualize it and pour it into Paul with all the love you feel for him. And every ounce of faith you have.'

Tam knelt beside the hospital bed to position herself more comfortably, her hand never leaving Paul's. Sophie Mandel knelt also, but both her hands covered Paul's one. She nodded weakly at Tam.

'Now shut your eyes and give Paul your energy. I'll do the same and tell you when to come out of it.' Tam watched her shut her eyes, then closed her own. She felt the subtle vibrations, the tingling in her body, and began to direct it to the unconscious boy. She prayed for his healing and his strength to defeat the coma.

Ten minutes later she felt that the boy had taken all the energy he could and further effort would be wasted. She slowly came out of the trance, then called across to Sophie Mandel to slowly break her contact.

Mrs. Mandel, opening her eyes, appeared in a greater fog than before, but her eyes were peaceful. 'I feel so much calmer now. It's as if the pain, the turmoil, has left me.'

'It's a restful state,' Tam told her. 'Sometimes the healer heals herself.'

They both stood up and, like clock-work, their eyes were drawn to Paul. He still slept on in his coma. Yet somehow, he, too, looked more peaceful. The aura of hopelessness had left the room.

Sophie Mandel bent down and kissed Paul's forehead. Then she and Tam went to join Asher in the waiting room. He stood up as they appeared. His eyes met Tam's, questioning her, wondering if she picked up any psychic data, but his lips never broached the subject.

'Can we give you a lift home, Mrs. Mandel?' he asked.

'No, thank you, Lieutenant. I'm staying in case Paul wakes up.'

Asher handed her his card. 'Will you call me if that happens? Any time of the day or night?'

'I will, Lieutenant Lowenstein. I'll get the nurse to phone you.' She turned to Tam. 'Tam, thank you. I don't know how, but you've given me strength, the strength to accept what's happened.'

'You've given it to yourself,' Tam answered and unexpectedly held out her arms. Sophie Mandel welcomed the hug.

'You have a child, too?' she asked.

'Yes.' Their eyes shared the pain but the fear had evaporated. Inner strength, Tam thought, to stand tall on life's most difficult paths.

Sophie Mandel's eyes filled and over-flowed. Yet she remained straight and calm.

'You'll be all right?' Asher asked.

The woman nodded.

'You're sure?'

'Yes. I need to be alone now, Lieutenant.'

'Please call me if you need me.'

'I will.'

Asher nodded.

'Bye,' Tam said, smiling, but feeling very tired and spent.

She and Ash turned and walked toward the elevators. As she glanced back, she saw Sophie Mandel sit on the couch in the waiting area, lean back and shut her eyes, perhaps to sleep, perhaps to pray.

'What did you pick up?' Asher asked as he gunned the motor and backed the car out of the parking space.

'Very little. I didn't probe. It's bad to

probe an injured or ill person's mind. Thoughts are energy and they need that energy to heal themselves. So I just sent him healing energy and since the path between our minds was open for that, I allowed any mental or verbal thoughts from him to travel across it.'

'And?'

'And, yes, I picked something up.'

When Tam lapsed into silence, Asher said, 'Take your time,' and drove through the quiet Northeast streets. Night had just fallen. It was just over six hours since the shooting. The muggy night had fewer people out and traffic was light.

Finally Tam, her voice wavering, said, 'I picked up the same image.' When Ash remained quiet, she continued, 'The same man I saw in my last meditation. For the Gambetti case.'

'The older man.'

'Yes.' She wavered again, as if trying to piece it together. 'It was only for a fleeting instant. But I think Paul saw his attacker for a moment. Then I registered pain and confusion. More confusion than pain.'

'The bullet severed an artery to the

heart. It hit him fast,' Ash agreed. 'Anything else?'

'Two words. 'No good.' They repeated themselves, over and over.' She looked quizzically at Asher. He shrugged his shoulder.

'Is the killer the same person, Tammy?' he asked her quietly.

She hesitated for only one instant. 'Yes, it's the same man. We're dealing with a serial murderer.'

'Shit,' Ash murmured as he turned down the quiet street Tam lived on. 'Do you think Mandel will come out of that coma, Tam?'

'He's holding on,' was all Tam could say. The car sidled into a space in front of Tam's home. The lights were on in the dining room of the first floor.

'If he comes to, we may have a witness.'

'We sent him a lot of healing.' She seemed to be speaking to some higher power, not him, as the crickets droned in the quiet Northeast greenery.

'Well, goodnight, Tam.' He bent over and affectionately pecked her cheek.

Tam turned toward him, abruptly. 'Will

you call me if he comes out of the coma?' Her eyes burned; she seemed to be in a trance. But it was more a state of intense and concentrated concern for those she tried to help. Ash had seen it before.

'I'll call you,' he said, and she knew he would.

Her face troubled, she gave him a hug and let herself out of the car. She looked at him for a minute through the car window, then abruptly turned and walked up the steps to her door. She didn't glance back as she opened it but disappeared silently through it. The door shut behind her.

Ash sighed, frustrated. He turned the key in the ignition, the car hummed properly and he drove away.

⋆   ⋆   ⋆

The telephone jangled him awake, Ash first thinking it was the alarm. But the velvet darkness outside eradicated that thought. His eyes scanned the clock face, 3:00 a.m., as he reached for the phone. 'Lowenstein here.'

'Lieutenant Lowenstein? This is the head nurse at the trauma unit at Jeanes. Mrs. Mandel asked me to call you. Paul Mandel is awake and lucid.'

'Tell her I'll be there in ten minutes. Thank you.' He hung up and reached for his trousers simultaneously.

He thought about calling Tam and decided to wait. He could call from the hospital.

* * *

Hospital corridors at 3:00 a.m. are hushed and haunting. Most patients have the good sense to sleep through the night, and any crisis is handled in a subdued manner that contrasts with the hustle and bustle of the day. Neither the dead nor dying may break the quietude of the graveyard shift. Hospital rules.

So Asher's 'I'm Lieutenant Lowenstein. Will you let Mrs. Mandel know I'm here?' to the night nurse sounded grotesquely loud in the shrouded silence.

'Shh!' She raised a finger to her lips. 'There are sick people here. I'll tell Mrs.

Mandel you're here.'

Asher wanted to laugh but restrained himself. He couldn't contain the excitement he felt at Paul Mandel's cheating death. If the boy could identify his attacker . . .

'Lieutenant Lowenstein?'

He whirled around at the faint soft voice.

Sophie Mandel stood there — exhausted, drawn, her hair slightly mussed — but her eyes and lips smiled. 'Paul's very weak but he can talk to you.'

★   ★   ★

Over an hour later, at 4:30 a.m., he phoned Tam. She answered groggily, but his words were a babble of excitement that woke her straight up. 'Paul Mandel came out of the coma, Tammy! He's weak but they let me talk to him. Tammy, he gave a description of the attacker — and it fits your description! He said the man was near a car when he came out into the parking lot; and when he looked at him, the man raised the gun and shot at him.

Paul said he tried to run for cover but there wasn't time. But that slight movement probably saved him from instant death. The medical report said the bullet penetrated the right lung about three inches from the heart. Paul said the man was close, about six yards away when he fired. I'm going to come back sometime tomorrow with a police artist and have them do up a composite sketch with Paul's help. Tam, he's a good kid. He's a really good kid.'

Tam, quiet through Asher's bubbling report, now asked, 'How is he feeling? What do the doctors say his condition is now?'

'He's still considered critical. I won't be able to spend a lot of time with him with Al.' Al was their top police artist. When there was still silence on Tam's end, he added, 'When I left, they had moved a small cot in for Sophie Mandel. They were both going to try to rest.'

'That's good.'

'Where's your enthusiasm, Tam?' He paused. 'You sound so reticent . . . is something wrong?'

'It's nearly 5:00 a.m.' Then, 'Yes, something's wrong. I sense he's still very sick, not out of danger yet. But that's probably less psychic input than *worried* input. But I'm going to send him some absentee healing energy before I go back to sleep. I'm glad he came out of it. Give him time to heal,' she added.

'I won't badger the kid, Tammy,' he assured her.

'Now who's watching old reruns of police shows? I mean, take it gentle; don't disturb the healing process.'

'I'll be gentle. Good night, Tam. I'll call you tomorrow.'

'Good night,' she said.

Asher hung up, set the alarm for 8:00 a.m. and fell into bed to recoup his sleep.

★　★　★

Tam fleetingly remembered being here before. David chugged down his orange juice in one great gulp. The boats along the river paraded gaily by their café table.

'Mom, do you mind if I go look

around?' David's voice was clear, sparkling.

'Be careful,' she said and he got up, eager and smiling.

She vaguely wondered where she was and then it registered. They were on board the *Moshulu*. She watched David climb backwards down the ladder to the lower deck. She sat and sipped her scotch and soda, feeling hazy.

Suddenly, she looked up. Asher had appeared, almost out of nowhere, leaning hard on the table. 'It's all right, Tam. It's all right. I'm here now.'

She stared at him quizzically for an instant, but his eyes stared deeply back into hers and he suddenly took off, climbing down to the lower decks as David had done.

The large report of a shot rang out. Tam felt ice in her veins. She moved, as if through heavy murk, and somehow reached the lower deck. She looked down at the blood-red iron deck. David lay sprawled out on his back. Shot. Tam felt the tears rise in a rush to her eyes.

And suddenly the scene faded into

darkness, and then the darkness took on shapes. The familiar outlines of her bedroom became visible in the faint morning light. Her alarm clock ticked rhythmically. Her eyes were wet. She craned her neck to see the time on the lighted dial. 5:20 a.m. She had been asleep less than a half hour.

She wiped her eyes and leaned back into the pillow. She knew David was safe, asleep in his bedroom across the hall. Yet this horrible dream, this horrible repetitive dream. Had it only returned because she had recalled it, earlier, in the hospital? Facing Paul Mandel's prone form? But Paul had recovered.

And the details were much sharper, clearer this time. Was it really getting to her, badly? Or was this dream an omen? She firmly cut the last thought, her eyes shut, praying, *Please, God, protect my son.* She believed in God, some Creator far superior to her, yet in contact with Its children. The prayer gave her solace and she let herself drift tiredly back to sleep.

It was just a dream. Just a dream.

But, dear God, it was getting to her.

Sunday Morning, July 14th

Asher slapped some aftershave on his face. He had called Al, who had promised to be over by 11:00 a.m. Then together, they'd proceed to the hospital to get Paul Mandel's description of his attacker.

The phone rang. Asher capped the aftershave and went to answer it.

* * *

Al sat, having rushed over to answer Asher's summons, drinking his coffee with all the animation of a cigar store Indian. His wiry unruly brown hair was still rumpled.

Asher stirred his coffee moodily. He slowly picked up the receiver of the phone in the kitchen and dialed. After three rings, a feminine voice answered. Breaking the utter quiet, Asher said, 'Tam . . . the hospital just called. Paul Mandel developed something called an

134

'overwhelming sepsis,' a serious blood infection resulting from the gunshot wound to his lung. They said it was rare for it to hit him this fast but it happens. Sophie Mandel asked if we'd come to the funeral.'

* * *

Tuesday, July 16th

The funeral procession, headlights on in the mid-morning light, wended its way through the Greater Northeast thorough-fares. Asher and Tam drove their car slowly behind the long serpent, funeral sticker displayed on the rear window. They were the eleventh and last car in line.

Roosevelt Memorial Park Cemetery in Trevose proved surprisingly cool for July. The black linen suit Asher wore did not have him bathing in buckets of sweat. Physically, he felt comfortable; emotion-ally, he was ice. He felt so sorry, so sorry, for Paul Mandel. If only they could have caught the bastard sooner. If only Paul hadn't had that fight with his Mom. If only . . .

If only they could get a lead on that murderous bastard . . .

Asher waited until the others had drifted away from the coffin. He threw the last flower on it. 'We'll catch him for you, Paul,' he said. He moved away, heading toward the cars. Tam stood with Sophie Mandel, their hands clasped in farewell. He approached Sophie Mandel discreetly. 'We'll catch him,' he promised in a low murmur.

The bereaved mother nodded, then her face puckered with a fresh onset of tears and grief. She turned to Tam. 'Can you contact the dead?' The tears traversed freely down her cheeks, spotting her black mourning dress.

'I can try.' Tam's voice remained steady despite her solemn face. 'If I can't, I can still help you to deal with it.'

'How much do you charge?' The question, apparently serious, was lightened by the brave attempt at a smile.

'Nothing,' Tam said. 'Thank me in

another way, if you choose.' Tam fished in her pocketbook for pen and paper and wrote down her name and number. She handed it to Sophie Mandel.

Asher saw the relatives and the funeral director waiting by the nearby cars. In the distance another car, gold-brown and medium-sized, pulled up. A young man got out. Perhaps a late arrival. Asher turned his gaze back to the mother. 'I guess we'll take our leave now, Sophie. Do you mind if I call you Sophie?'

Sophie Mandel inclined her head in a gracious gesture. 'Please.'

Asher reached out to take her hands and squeezed them lightly.

'Lieutenant Lowenstein? Mrs. Mandel?' It was the latecomer. 'I'm Walt Morris from the *Daily News*.'

He was followed by another man Ash hadn't seen emerge from the car, who now raised a camera to his left eye.

A flash bulb went off in their faces.

A chill rage surged in Ash. 'Mr. Morris, this is not the time.'

'I'm sorry, Lieutenant. I'm on assignment. The city wants to know if this and

137

the last murder were connected. Is this why the lieutenant is here, Mrs. Mandel?' He cocked his tablet and pencil in Sophie Mandel's direction. She stared at him as if he were a worm that had crawled from out the grave.

'Tam, take Sophie over to the cars.'

As Tam guided her away, the reporter pointed his pencil at her, opening his mouth to speak. Asher placed a hand on his shoulder, slowly applying pressure. 'You can speak to me,' he both offered and commanded.

The eager beaver took the hint, struggling to regain his professional decorum. Asher released his grasp and lowered his hand. He wondered if the city desk was swarming with phone calls from anxious parents and if Morris had been told to catch them off guard and get something, anything, to print. 'What makes you think they're connected?' he asked.

'An anonymous tip we received,' Morris replied.

Buehl, Asher thought, but he hadn't any real evidence. He dropped the thought.

'Aside from that,' Morris continued, 'we added two and two. The murders were just over one week apart, each victim a teenage boy living with a single parent. It sounded reasonable to assume there might be a connection.'

'Don't you know that might add up to five, Mr. Morris? The murders might not be connected. We have no real — ' Asher hesitated just an instant too long and Morris finished the line for him.

'Proof, Lieutenant? Then you are considering it.'

Ash suddenly felt tired. He knew the public had the right to know, but its lifelong fascination with speculation wearied him. And he couldn't commit to a statement without proof. 'Mr. Morris,' he hedged, 'the Philadelphia Police Department will consider every possible lead. That includes the possibility that they're separate murders, similar but unrelated. Now, if you'll excuse me, I have to get back to my partner.' He walked quickly away, ignoring Morris's call of 'Lieutenant?' and joined Tam, waiting in the car.

No other cars, save his and the

reporter's, were left, Asher saw with grim satisfaction. Sophie Mandel had gotten safely away to sit Shivah, to mourn for the loss of her son.

7

Asher had foregone lunch, drinking coffee instead as he read the autopsy and ballistics report on the late Paul Mandel. Ballistics confirmed it: the gun used on Paul was a .22 caliber pistol, the same caliber used to murder Nicky Gambetti. Ash glanced at the digital clock on his desk, feeling light-headed, wondering if he should've forced himself to eat something. He and Tam had courteously declined Sophie Mandel's invitation to stop by, to partake of the traditional refreshments her family and friends would serve during Shivah. It was better that she should mourn in peace, and her family be spared from casting the inevitable glances his way.

The clock ticked toward 3:00 p.m. Feeling exhausted, Asher considered visiting the nearby deli luncheonette. Something light. Maybe a tuna sandwich and a coke. He got up and headed for the elevator. He would stop at the lunchroom where Colby had gone for a soda, to tell him he'd be gone for an hour.

Some commotion was going on in the lobby as he stepped off the elevator. And as he moved past the circular column to look, he wondered: had the Devil himself planned this fiasco to torment him exclusively?

For both Walter Buehl from *ad nauseam* and Walt Morris from the *Daily News*, the latter's photographer trailing behind him, vied loudly in the lobby for Dennis Colby's attention, apparently unaware they were on the same hell-bent mission.

The front desk sergeant frowned on the erupting chaos. He appealed to Colby, who had, coke in hand, walked into it, to straighten the noisy visitors out.

'Excuse me, I was here first,' Buehl said, his tone frosted, polite but firm.

'Yeah. Three steps ahead,' Morris drawled back. He looked like a bird ready to peck, tiny and bony with a belligerent beak nose.

But Walter Buehl was staring at the

camera in the other man's hand. Morris took advantage of this hiatus and whipped out his pad. 'Excuse me, Sergeant Colby? I'm Walt Morris from the *Daily News*.'

Buehl's eyebrows rose. 'You're from the newspaper?'

Dennis Colby spoke in a firm but fierce voice, his patience gone. 'I don't care if either one of you is from hell and back. If you both don't calm down, I'm going to throw you both out of here.' They stared silently back at him and Asher, behind him, chuckled silently. 'Now. One at a time. You first.' He deliberately pointed at Morris with a steady, no-nonsense finger.

Walter Morris looked up, caught Asher standing quietly and, in a subdued voice, said, 'Hello, Lieutenant Lowenstein.'

Sergeant Colby glanced around, acknowledged Ash and pivoted back to face Morris with a hard stare.

The reporter smoothly returned his attention to Colby, who waited with an air of renewed patience. 'The press believes there's reasonable evidence to connect the two recent murders of Paul

Mandel and Nicky Gambetti.' Morris's stance was casual but professional. 'I'm here to get the Department's viewpoint on that.'

Buehl cut in before Colby had a chance to take a breath. 'Mr. Morris, I believe I have evidence as to who the killer of these young boys is!'

Morris glanced at him and laughed. 'Oh, yeah? Well, I have to get the official police line on that.' He sized Buehl up for an interesting nut and turned back to Colby. 'Well, Sergeant?'

Colby grimaced. 'I'm not in charge of this investigation.'

'Oh, that's right. Lieutenant Lowenstein is.' He stared steadfastly at Asher, who returned the gaze so unblinkingly that Morris had to break the stare for a moment. 'Well, Lieutenant? The people really want to know.' As Asher hesitated, he added, 'We've been getting phone calls. Parents are beginning to wonder if there's some maniac teen-killer on the loose.'

'Mr. Morris,' Asher said in a tone of real regret, 'I don't have any authority yet to give such information. The lab is still compiling the latest data, and even when it does complete it, the final authority is handed down from Captain Frank Anunzio, not me.'

'I'm here, Ash,' came a voice behind him. Anunzio walked over to the lobby desk and nodded to the desk sergeant, who resumed his other duties. 'Mr. Morris,' Anunzio addressed the reporter, 'the lab has confirmed its findings and there will be a press conference held tomorrow at 2:00 p.m. in the auditorium here at the Roundhouse.'

'Can't you give me something for now, Captain?'

Anunzio pursed his lips in a thoughtful gesture. 'Now, that wouldn't be fair, would it? But you do have a scoop of sorts. The other media won't learn about the press conference till 9:00 a.m. tomorrow. We would like to get at least one good night's sleep. You can rehash the known facts in your morning edition with the scheduled press conference added. Capeesh?'

Morris nodded, his lips edging into an

appreciative smile. 'See you at two tomorrow, Captain.'

Anunzio gave the reporter a mock 'at ease' salute. Morris cocked his head at his photographer. They silently exited the building. Buehl still remained. Anunzio turned his attention to him. 'Walter, come with me.' As Buehl eagerly responded, the captain turned to Asher. 'You, too.'

He's seen the description Paul Mandel gave, Asher thought, and knows it *could* fit Tony Buehl. But it could fit Walter Buehl, too, and a hundred older men like him. Was Anunzio seriously considering Walter Buehl's obsession?

What was the captain up to?

In Anunzio's sparse office, the captain seated Walter Buehl in the guest chair to the left and Asher in the one to the right. Then he eased himself into his own cushioned seat behind the desk.

'Walter,' he began, 'we understand your concern for your brother and his possible involvement in some crime.' He waved Buehl, who had begun to rise excitedly from his chair, back into his seat. 'But even if he *is* involved in these murders, going public with a picture of him as a major suspect is bad police business without proof. We'd need to be sure he was the murderer and have a warrant for his arrest. It's also bad timing. It will scare him off, make him go into hiding. We want him visible, where we can nab him. I, too, would like to settle his role in this one way or another.'

Buehl, placated, nodded. 'So how do you propose to find him? Before he commits another murder.'

'Via television coverage,' Anunzio answered, glancing at Asher, who remained rock-still in his chair. 'In fact, we're going to put two bulletins on TV. One will broadcast a police composite of the unknown killer of those boys, based on the last victim's description of the killer and another confidential source.' He raised his eyebrows at Buehl's questioning expression at the word 'confidential.' Buehl backed down visibly, sitting quietly once more. 'We will ask the public to supply any information they can that might aid the police department in their apprehension of this man.'

'But what about my brother?' Walter

Buehl cut in tersely.

'I'm coming to that. Separately, we will release another story reporting Tony's escape from the State hospital, describing him, asking anyone who has knowledge of his whereabouts to inform the police. Please note, Walter, we cannot state that Tony is dangerous, only that he's childlike and may become agitated upon apprehension, according to his doctor.'

'But he can be dangerous!'

'Walter, I'm your friend. You can trust me. I can only authorize the known facts to be broadcast. Hopefully, this will get Tony found and returned to the hospital. Then any further connection can be found out, if it exists.'

Walter Buehl bristled but nodded curtly. 'It sounds like a good plan.'

'Thank you.' Anunzio turned to Asher. 'Lieutenant Lowenstein, I want to see you in my office at 10:00 a.m. tomorrow to get all the details on both broadcast bulletins. Please tell Ms. Westington I'd also like to see her here. She may be helpful.'

'Yes, Captain. Shouldn't be a problem.

148

She's currently between temp jobs.'

Buehl looked curious at the mention of Ms. Westington but as no one offered further commentary, he appeared to swallow the question on his lips. Apparently, he was getting what he wanted and was satisfied. For now. Instead he asked, 'When will the bulletins be broadcast, Frank?'

Anunzio permitted the familiarity, although it appeared his former acquaintance with this man was now strained. 'Tomorrow night. *The Six O'Clock News.*'

Buehl nodded, satisfied again. Then abruptly he asked, 'You'll keep me informed?'

'Of course.' Anunzio rose. 'Well, gentlemen, shall we adjourn this meeting for now?'

Buehl rose to meet him. 'Thank you, Frank. Call me if you need me in the slightest way.'

Anunzio inclined his head in the slightest way, a small nod. As Asher rose, Buehl turned to him uncertainly. 'Thank you, Lieutenant,' he said, and he extended his hand with a touch of hesitation.

Asher shook it briefly, masking his distaste, then addressed Anunzio. 'Captain, I'll be at my desk if you need me.'

'Dismissed.'

He exited the Captain's office, noting that Buehl still stood there, obviously reluctant to leave; then the man finally and stiffly left. Ash walked swiftly back to his desk and sat woodenly down, wondering if Tony Buehl, wherever he was, would think he was a suspect for murders he may not have committed, once those bulletins were released. Separate coverage or not, many people would link them. Was a witch-hunt on? Was Anunzio aware such dual coverage might create one? Where was Tony Buehl, and was he involved?

His reverie was interrupted as Anunzio came over to his desk. The captain smiled sagely. 'I understand you haven't eaten yet, Lieutenant. Come on, let's get a bite. And get the hell out of here for a while.'

Asher smirked up at his superior. Obviously Dennis Colby was observant as usual and had clued in the captain.

'Sounds good to me,' he said. He hoped the deli's tuna was still fresh.

$$\star \quad \star \quad \star$$

Wednesday, July 17th

The auditorium at Headquarters served as a small but adequate meeting hall. A raised platform toward the back comprised the stage, and a podium with a built-in microphone sat centered in front upon it. The clock neared 2:00 p.m.; personnel had arranged folding chairs for the press and tested the small sound system.

The reporters with their pads and pencils, photographers with their Minoltas, and TV people with their minicams had piled into the room. The buzz of the newspeople was loud; the yellow lighting bathing the room, bright and glaring.

A side door just past the front row of seats opened and the attention of the mingling crowd turned its way. Cameras, minicams and eyes swiveled to follow

Frank Anunzio's trail to the podium. Asher Lowenstein followed him.

'Gentlemen.' The captain opened with a slight bow. 'Ladies. The Philadelphia Police Department has been investigating the recent murders of Nicholas Gambetti and Paul Mandel. And although they occurred in opposite ends of this city, we have reason to believe they may be connected.' A rustled murmur ran through the tightened throng as they clustered closer, poised for questions at the first opening break. They reminded the captain of race horses at the starting line, pawing but patient, racing by the rules. Silence returned. Anunzio continued.

'In both instances, the murder victims were teenaged boys living in a single-parent home with their mothers, and in both instances, an argument between each boy and his respective mother preceded the fatal attacks. The mothers in both cases were not witness to the actual murder and their involvement has been totally ruled out. Therefore, the modus operandi is the same for both: a killer stalking his victim after possibly overhearing a loud parent-child dispute.

'Further investigation shows that the murderer may or may not be from either neighborhood. He may have been visiting one or the other and apparently the volatile argumentative setting may be a trigger setting him on a path of emotional violence.'

A hand shot up in the second row. Anunzio acknowledged it.

A young woman with wavy auburn hair stood. 'Captain, you said 'he.' Do you have reason to believe the murderer is a man?'

Anunzio nodded. 'Yes. We have a basic description given to our investigative officer, Lieutenant Lowenstein, by Paul Mandel, the second victim, before he died.'

'Do you have any hard proof of this connection, Captain?' The dark-haired man in the front row shot a mike toward the captain as he spoke.

'Yes,' Anunzio answered. 'Most definitely, but we're not able to divulge that information at this time.'

The lab had released a new report: the .22 caliber pistol the killer used, an older model, had a defect. There was a minute misalignment of the cylinder and the barrel. The bullet, coming out of the chamber, scraped with infinitesimal pressure against the barrel for an instant before it propelled outward from the gun. Both bullets had the same pressure mark, barely visible to the naked eye but clearly delineated by the lab.

'Why is he doing this?' an older man called out. 'Have you determined a motive yet?'

'The only motive we have to date is a possible psychological one. The mother-son fights apparently trigger, as I've said, something in the killer, drawing him to the source of the argument, centering his aggression on the boy in each case, but not the mother. This is simply stating the facts. We're not drawing a conclusion.'

'Captain Anunzio!' Asher recognized the sharp features and eager expression of Walt Morris from the *News*. 'Would you say these boys were troubled, emotionally disturbed?'

'I don't get your point.'

'Well, if the arguments were loud enough to draw the killer's attention and trigger the psychological response, they must have been very serious violent arguments. Were the mothers hurt in either instance?'

'They were *loud* arguments in both cases. Neither of the mothers was injured in any way.'

'By their sons?'

'No. I still don't get your point, Mr . . .'

'Morris. My point is: did the killer think he was protecting the mother?'

'We have no reason to believe that, Mr. Morris. The boys were shot after the arguments occurred. I'm sorry, but that comes under the heading of speculation.'

'My business,' Walt Morris conceded with a quirky grin.

But something in Asher's brain clicked on and an elusive wheel began to turn, round and round, examining Morris's speculative question. Then the connection came: the fight over forty years ago between Tony Buehl and his doomed mother. But, Asher thought as Anunzio handed out composite sketches of the murder suspect and wrapped up the session with news of the six o'clock broadcasts, Tony Buehl was not protecting his mother but attacking her; and, according to Dr. Robbins's file, the then-young Walter Buehl happened onto the murder scene long after whatever argument had triggered Mrs. Buehl's death.

Was Tony a potential suspect? Was he wandering about, hearing a recreation of his violence from long ago and trying to save these women in lieu of the mother he lost in heated passion years ago? Somehow attacking the modem versions of his earlier self in a frenzy of restitution?

Speculation or not, it might be possible, despite Dr. Robbins's assurances. Maybe he should run it by the good doctor.

But one last question nagged. How did an escaped mental patient with a childlike nature get and learn how to handle a gun? A highly unlikely connection after all. Yet it nagged at his brain, something right but not right about Morris's assumption.

The elusive wheel began to turn again, this time repetitiously, teasing but evading an answer. Asher let it go. Insights in criminology sometimes sat behind doors barred from within. If he didn't force it, an answer might emerge on its own.

* * *

The late afternoon paper gave the murderer a distinctive title that was picked up gleefully by the *Six O'Clock News* broadcast. It played up the fact that both murdered boys were products of a disrupted family environment: one, through the death of his father; the other, through divorce. Especially in the case of Nicky Gambetti, the simple word 'blue' became a synonym for teenage loneliness, estrangement and death.

'POLICE SEARCH FOR TROUBLED TEENS' MURDERER,' the front page blared, 'CITY ROCKED BY THE BABY BOY BLUE KILLER!'

Inside, Walt Morris's article drew the correlations between the murder victims' home lives and the killer's strange appearance, 'like a warped savior,' following heated family conflicts. Morris was generously helped by Mrs. Anna Gambetti, whom he had interviewed that morning before the Philly P.D. press conference. Mrs. Gambetti had apparently needed to talk to someone and Walt Morris supplied his readership with a tight, detailed story.

By evening's end everyone was discussing the Baby Boy Blue Killer, and mothers in Philadelphia took pains to speak quietly to their teenage sons. The number of family arguments fell faster than the Dow Jones on a bad day on Wall Street.

★　★　★

Tam turned on the TV for the *Six O'Clock News*. David, sitting at the table in the dining area off the living room, lifted his head from the novel on his summer reading list to watch.

'Are they going to have it on?' he asked.

'Yes.'

'Who do you think the killer is, Mom?'

'I don't know yet, David. My description matched Paul Mandel's but we don't know who this man is yet.'

'That's a shame about Paul Mandel.' David shook his head. 'He almost made it.'

Tam said nothing but her shoulders and chest heaved with a large sigh. David knew it still upset her. 'Are you still going to see Mrs. Mandel?' he asked.

'Yes. Sometime next week.'

'You know, you *should* charge for it.'

'David!' Tam turned an angry glance on him, then checked herself.

'All right, all right! It's just that other people do.'

'It's just not my way. I don't even like taking the stipend the Department pays me per case. I only agreed to get Asher off *my* case.'

'Yeah, and you sent your last paycheck from the Philly P.D. off to a charity. Mom . . . doctors get paid for helping people. They don't say, 'It's a gift from God.''

'Doctors attend schools for many years. Shush now. It's coming on.'

'So go to a school for psychics,' David laughed, joining her on the living room sofa. He caught her affectionate smirky side-glance, complete with raised eyebrow, and gave her a wicked grin.

Then they turned back to the TV as the composite sketch of the killer flashed onto the screen.

★   ★   ★

There was stunned silence. Santa, Claire, Murphy, Annie Belle and Scrugs gathered closer to the small TV set. Tony stayed frozen on the couch.

They'd been watching the news because of Santa Ana's interest in the MOVE fiasco. He wasn't too keen on the MOVE members — 'They shouldn't have hassled their neighbors, man.'; and definitely not on the police action — 'A bomb, man? They should've known better. A bulldozer would've done it and no one hurt bad. Violence is never good, man. It screwed both sides up.' But the tragedy intrigued him. He wanted to know the truth, as did many people in Philadelphia. But for Santa, the truth went beyond the facts. Was some larger karmic debt involved? Would the City's aura heal? Would some good come of it, out of the bad?

The group became used to Santa turning on the news broadcasts for the latest developments. Lately, they watched together and discussed it afterwards with him. Searching, as ever, for truth. But tonight, a different truth assaulted them.

'Dear God, that sketch looks like Tony!' Annie Belle wasn't afraid to say what they each were thinking. She didn't actually believe it was Tony.

'That's me!' Tony gasped, and cringed. 'They're looking for me!' He looked at them, wild-eyed. 'Walt's looking for me! He did this! I know, I know!'

Claire was beside him immediately. 'It's just a coincidence. Calm down, Tony. This isn't about you at all. They're looking for a killer. A lot of people might fit that man's face.'

The TV anchorman wrapped up the Baby Boy Blue Killer portion of his broadcast and went on to the next story.

'But you guys said it was me.' Tony

began to shiver, his arms folded protectively against himself, his fingers pressing
hard into his shoulders.

'No, Tony. We only said it looked like
you.'

'Claire.' Santa Ana's voice hushed them
both and the anchorman's broadcast
came through all too clearly.

' . . . escaped from the State Hospital
on July 2nd. Both the police and the
hospital's efforts to locate Tony Buehl
have, to date, failed. Again, he is not
considered dangerous, but may be
unstable emotionally. If you have any
information on the whereabouts of Tony
Buehl, please contact the Philadelphia
Police Department. Again, he is described
as being fifty-one years old, five feet seven
inches in height, thinly built, with brown
eyes, and is partially bald with sparse
brown hair. He may also appear confused
and childlike. Any information at all
could be helpful.'

The anchorman smoothly handed the
program over to his sportscaster.

Santa Ana shut the TV off, roughly.
'Jesus Christ. They are looking for you.'

'What are we going to do?' Claire's voice was calm; it was a question. If hearts thumped, there were no hysterics. Tony was their friend, a family member. They would reach a decision calmly, through love. Claire's gaze was on Santa, but he turned to the rest of them, his own gaze asking silently for answers.

'We should meditate,' Annie said gravely. 'Then we'll watch the *Eleven O'Clock News* . . . with clearer heads.'

Tony had been taught meditation. He joined them as eyes shut, bodies slumped and minds relaxed and opened. Absolute quiet reigned in the house on Coulter Street for the next hour.

Claire got up first and headed for the kitchen to start some coffee perking. Annie blinked heavily, the sound of Claire's movement bringing her awake. Her eyes caught Santa's, sitting quietly across from her. Scrugs was still meditating, Tony stock-still beside him, his tears also silent. Murphy stirred beside Annie, rose and walked over to Tony. He placed his hand on Tony's shoulder. 'Come on, let's get some coffee.' His voice jarred

Scrugs, frowning and troubled, out of his meditation.

'Coffee will be ready soon,' Claire told them. They all filed to the table.

'I think Tony's being framed.' Scrugs spoke finally. 'I'm not sure, but I think maybe he is.'

'Why do you say that?' Annie Belle asked, though they all knew where he was heading. Best to let Scrugs say it. He knew, better than any of them, what being framed was like.

'It's just the way they ran those stories. First, they're looking for a killer and the killer looks like Tony; and then they're looking for Tony.'

'I ain't no killer,' Tony said plaintively.

'I know you're not,' Scrugs said with an unaccustomed softness.

'I think you're speculating, man,' Santa said. 'Maybe they just ran it that way. Not connecting anything.'

'People are going to think it's Tony,' Claire interposed, bringing out the coffee. 'People are going to start wondering about the 'escaped mental patient.''

'They got no right to call him a mental

patient,' Murphy muttered. 'Tony's cool. He's not nuts. He's just been hurt bad from what happened . . . long ago. He paid for it in spades.'

'Claire's right, though,' Santa interjected glumly. 'Between the sketch and them looking for Tony, we can't take him out. It's gonna be like prison for him here.'

'Prison?' Tony looked at them desperately. 'No, you're my friends. It's okay. I'll hide here!'

Annie Belle broke the pervading silence. 'Tony, you're not hiding. Not here. Not anywhere.'

'We're gonna clear your name,' Santa Ana decided. He knew Tony didn't understand and added, 'We're gonna tell the truth and get you free.'

'I was free.'

'You still are,' Annie soothed.

'But they'll make me go back. To the hospital.'

Silence again, then Scrugs said, 'We won't desert you, Tony.'

'We'll get you back,' Murphy said and Annie Belle, beside him, nodded.

'I was in trouble,' Scrugs confided, 'and

they didn't desert me. Some creep planted cocaine on me and set me up for a bust to pay me back for something he thought I did. Santa stood by me till they cleared my name and helped me put it behind me. Now we're gonna clear your name and help you through it.'

'No matter what it takes,' Annie added.

'Truth, man,' Santa Ana said, 'we're gonna tell the truth. And we won't let them lock you up again. If we need to, we'll get a lawyer.' He looked at Claire, who nodded.

Tony took a moment, thinking how to say it. 'I'm still scared. But if you guys stand by me . . . ' His voice trailed off.

'We'll be there,' Claire told him, and the others nodded agreement. 'But we've got to straighten it out.'

'We'll watch the *Eleven O'Clock News*,' Santa said, 'and then we'll make a final decision on how to handle it.'

★ ★ ★

At 11:30 p.m., a decision was reached. Tony balked but they convinced him it

166

was best to go to police headquarters. They thought at first to tackle it in the morning, but Annie had a sudden insight. 'The morning will be bad. We have to go now.' When they pressed her for surety, she would not back down. 'I sense disaster in the morning. We have to go now.'

They were tired and Tony pleaded out of fear for one more night. But Annie Belle was adamant. They got on their jackets and started up the station wagon.

'Come on, Tony,' Santa Ana said as he led him protectively to the car. 'It ain't gonna change in the morning.'

8

It had just been a hunch. Sometimes
Asher followed them, sometimes he
didn't. Tonight he had, and it didn't yield
a shred of useful information. It had
started with a chance remark over the
phone with Tam at 8:00 p.m. Working
late, still concerned over the coinciding
coverage on the killer and Tony Buehl, he
had said, 'You know, though, the
description does fit Tony Buehl.'

'From what you've told me of his
brother,' Tam had answered, 'it could fit
Walter Buehl.'

'Any vibes?' he had asked.

Tam had hesitated. 'Only chills,' she
said. 'But I could be picking that up from
you. I know you detest the man.'

'With good cause,' Ash replied, 'with
good cause.'

But after the conversation, the
younger Buehl still lingered in his mind.
Asher threw on his coat, jumped in his

car and drove to nearby Society Hill. Acting on that hunch. He parked down the street from Buehl's swank apartment building.

Thirty minutes later, Walter Buehl emerged from the building, walked to its small parking lot and entered his own car. Ash appreciated the fact that Buehl was a slow and careful driver. It made it easier to trail him from a distance unseen. He followed Buehl off I-95 at the Bridge Street exit and up to a veteran's hall in the Wissinoming neighborhood in the Northeast.

Buehl parked his car and entered the hall. Fifteen minutes later, Asher made some discreet inquiries of others entering it, and found out Buehl was speaking to a local business association on the banker's role in assisting small businesses with mortgages and loans. No illegal activity there. Sometimes hunches paid. Sometimes, like tonight, they didn't.

Getting in his car, Asher drove to Bustleton Avenue, disgruntled but thankful for one thing. At least the fruitless shadowing had headed him back home.

Pete Delaney trudged up the street to Torresdale Avenue. He continued on to the bar at the corner of Torresdale and Bridge Street. He had made this short journey on many a warm night, usually around midnight.

He called it his mother's witching hour. About when she couldn't hold her liquor anymore. During the winter, she did her drinking at home, where he and his stepfather could keep a lid on it or force her to sleep it off after the witching hour. He wished she would go to A.A. But no matter how hard he and Joe pleaded, she clung to the bottle like a kid with a teddy bear.

At first, neighborhood friends who frequented the bar would walk or drag her home, depending on how feisty she got. But he and Joe put a stop to that. They told Pearl, the barmaid, and Sonny, the owner, that either Joe or he would be there regular at midnight to tow her home; and if she started fading earlier, to call them.

But midnight was the witching hour, the hour Mary Delaney always seemed to go under.

Lately, Pete went to claim her. Joe was getting on in years and not as strong. It was a trade-off. Although Joe could get her to come quietly, if she stumbled it was hard on him to lift her along. Pete was muscular and capable of supporting his mother the few blocks home. But she resented him doing it and, once past the bar and her drinking buddies, her mouth flew and her drunken arms flailed. He had to fight her home, controlling his anger.

The last part was easier. He wanted to cry for his mother. She was going to kill herself and leave them mourning the life she threw away. Sometimes he wanted to cry for himself and Joe. He didn't know how a fifteen-year-old kid was supposed to get through it and pass school and all that. He couldn't even bring his friends home.

He reached the open door to the tavern. Through it, he could see her, her head lolling, dangerously close to her glass, held lightly against the counter. With her slender figure and her long blonde hair, red-highlighted, masking her face, she looked young and vulnerable. He moved aside to let two older men exit through the opened doorway. They were wearing suits despite the heat, which even late night breezes off the nearby Delaware River hadn't cooled.

Pete steeled himself and went into the bar, catching Sonny's look. The brawny man moved behind the counter, gave a customer his beer, then sidled confidently over to Pete's mother. He whispered something to her then looked again in Pete's direction. His mother looked, too, but her face didn't wear the amiable smile that Sonny's did. She was teed and it creased her features, aging them, destroying the earlier illusion.

Pete walked slowly over to her. 'Mom? You ready to go?'

'Nah. I haven't finished my scotch.'

'Well, drink it up and we'll go home. You know how lonely Joe gets without you.'

His mother apparently didn't hear him.

'You wanna drink?'

'Mom, you know I can't drink.'

'Why not? Idz good for you.'

Pete calmed himself, pushing the frustration from her last remark out of his mind. 'Mom, I'm underage.'

'Oh. Oh, yeah. Well, don't worry. Your day'll come. Then you can have a drink.' She turned and smiled up at him, her eyes bleary. The small shift in movement on her barstool did the trick. She started to fall backwards, the glass in her hand spilling its golden brown liquor. Pete caught her and straightened her up. He kept a protective hand on her shoulder.

Mary Delaney stared at the remaining dregs of scotch. 'Oh!'

'Come on, Mom. Let's go.'

'Lemme finish my drink.' She downed the last gulp, put the glass down regretfully and waved to the people in the bar. 'Goo'bye, folks!'

They all made the correct gestures and Pete helped his mother through the crowded bar and out onto the empty sidewalk. She waited until they were halfway down the block on Torresdale. He

173

knew it was coming by the pursing of her lips and the stiffening of her limbs.

'So you think I'm a God-damned drunk!' It came out in a mutter and she pushed away from him. Or tried to. He held her tight and held his own tongue. A parked car a few feet up revved its motor. Mary Delaney pulled and strained against Pete's strong grip. 'Help!' she shouted. 'Help me! Make him leave me go!'

The man in the car's darkened interior seemed to stare at them. Pete gave his mother an exasperated frown. He spoke in a soft, barely controlled voice. 'Mom, you're embarrassing me. I'm only trying to take you home.'

'Home!' she spat. 'You're treatin' me like a child. I'm a grownup, Petey. I can have a coupla shots!'

'You can't hold your booze!' he seethed between clenched teeth, his tension breaking. 'You're a lush and you won't get help!'

His body shook with a pent-up fury and the shaking loosened his grip. His mother broke away, swaying uncertainly, moving with some last reserve of energy to the corner. She started across the small street but Pete caught up, grasped her firmly and pointed her down the side street. 'This way, Mom.' He felt numb and crazy, aware and scared that, for the first time, tears were escaping from his eyes. Shit! Guys his age weren't supposed to cry! But he wanted to . . . wanted to for too long now.

This was *it!* He and Joe would have to force her into therapy. He was thankful they were down the block from their house and was thankful he heard that driver behind them pull out to leave. He didn't need some well-meaning Good Samaritan interfering. Once she told a passing stranger he wasn't her son but a punk harassing her. And the guy nearly believed her. Lucky it was right outside the bar and Sonny saw what was happening.

His mother writhed against him, whispering obscene invective.

'That's right, Mom. We're close to home. Keep it low.'

It was the wrong thing to say. Her eyes

glared, her teeth clenched. Her head swiveled wildly as she stared into the night. 'Help! Help! He's got me! He's gonna kill me! Help! Help!'

'Mom, goddammit!' he was shouting and couldn't help it. They were two doors away from home. A couple of neighboring lights went on, but they saw it was him and his mother and knew the noise would stop shortly. 'You see that, Mom? You're waking the neighbors!'

'Let me go. I can walk myself to the door.'

'No, you can't. You got steps to climb.'

'Bitch!' Mary Delaney screamed, 'You're no good! You're a bitchin' no good kid, treatin' me this way!' She railed against his grasp. 'I hate you!'

'No, you don't, Mom.'

The screen door opened and Pete breathed a sigh of worn relief. Joe traveled down the steps in the darkness; they kept the porch light off both for privacy and for Mary's sake. 'Come on, Mary. I got ya. Let's go in and get some rest.'

'Joe, we got to stop this,' Pete said, panting.

'Joe, he tried to hurt me. He's tryin' to hurt me!'

'No, Mary, he's tryin' to help you. We're both tryin' to help you.'

They got Mary into bed. She turned her face to the wall, away from them.

Joe led his stepson out into the living room. 'I got an A.A. representative comin' over day after tomorrow. She's gonna talk to her.'

'How 'bout tomorrow night?'

'She ain't goin' to that bar, Petey, even if I have to tie her down. I'm gonna talk to Sonny, too. Maybe he can help somehow. Steer her out of there. He must be thinkin' of it himself. She's never been this bad.'

'Yes, she has, Joe. You just didn't wanta see it.'

'Maybe you're right. Maybe you're right, Petey.'

Pete felt the tears welling up again and was glad for the darkness. 'Look, Joe. I just wanta sit by myself on the porch for a while. Okay?'

There was a moment's hesitation, as if Joe was weighing the heavy silence between them. 'Okay. I'll be here if you need me.'

Pete nodded, opened the screen door and went out. He sat down in the outdoor lounge chair, letting the quiet of the night wash over him. He knew Joe would sit likewise on the sofa inside, waiting until he came back in, ready for bed. There was that about Joe . . . he cared about people. Shame Joe hadn't married his mother years ago, before it got too hard on her and she turned to the sauce.

He hoped Joe meant it. About putting a stop to all this crap.

Pete shook his head, trying to clear it, to retreat back into the still darkness, lit only by a few streetlamps. He saw a man walking up the street, well-dressed. Going somewhere despite the late hour. Pete watched him blindly, without interest. Until he started up their front steps. Pete stared at him curiously: an older man, probably fifty. 'Mister, who are you looking for?'

'You're no good. You're a no-good kid and you oughta be dead!' The man drew a gun as Pete watched, horrified. Then instinct took over and his body moved into flight.

It seemed he had just begun to bolt away when a searing pain cut into his upper left side. A hot throbbing ran from his chest to his shoulder. He felt nauseous and wanted to collapse, but the instinct to run was greater. He groped in quickened terror for the porch railing, seeing the gun raise again from the corner of his eye. His only thought was *Jesus, Mary, Mother O' God*.

'Pete. What's happening out he — ' As the porch light went on, Joe's voice faded from shock. He gaped at the man with the gun.

The man aimed the gun wildly. It apparently fired, although no sound but a harsh metallic pop was heard. The bullet burst through the screen door, missing Joe and ricocheting into the mirror on the wall behind him. The mirror shattered with a loud crash.

The man seemed confused, about to lift the gun again, when the next-door neighbor's screen door opened and her porch light blazed on. 'What's going on here?' The elderly woman gazed through her half-opened screen door.

'Mrs. Wells, get back! He's got a gun!'

But before Mrs. Wells could react, the man bolted down the steps, ran to a car and drove off with tires screeching.

Joe knelt beside Pete where he had fallen against the railing. He was bleeding badly and Joe ripped his shirt off to use it to stanch the blood.

'I'll call for an ambulance,' Mrs. Wells said, snapping out of her shock.

'And the police,' Joe shouted. He continued to work against the blood flow. So intently he didn't hear their screen door open.

Pete, half-conscious, saw his mother staring wide-eyed at them. Joe followed his gaze and turned to see Mary, too.

She suddenly clasped her hand to her mouth, her gorge obviously rising, and ran to the bathroom to relieve herself, to cleanse herself, of the night's debauchery and its horror.

★   ★   ★

A motley crew.

The small hodgepodge group had straggled warily into the Roundhouse lobby, saying they were there about the TV broadcast. Colby had been called down to check them out.

They edged hesitantly toward him. Moments like this, Colby thought, made pulling late shift desk duty anything but dull.

He studied the six of them. First, the two women: one, a short dark-haired beauty with intense flaming eyes; the other, a willowy quiet blonde, not beautiful but not bad-looking either. Then the men — an odd assortment if ever he saw one. First, a heavy-duty guy who looked like he could double as Jerry Garcia at a Grateful Dead concert; then a skinny short guy who'd probably feel at home in a Dickens novel; along with a tall, hard-muscled bald guy who could easily top the bill at an all-star wrestling match. And the last guy: he was the *piece de resistance*. Not too tall, partially bald, and obviously older than the others. He was crying like a little kid while the rest of them comforted him.

And they shuffled in at around midnight. Perfect timing.

Colby spread his hands in an amiable gesture. 'You folks say you have some information on the TV broadcast?'

The tiny brunette came forward. She seemed to be searching for words, then swallowed and began. 'Please, officer, we're here to do what's right but we need your help, too. This gentleman has become our good friend.' She indicated the shaky older guy. 'We met him about two weeks ago and he didn't have a place to stay or people to care for him. He told us his brother was keeping him locked up . . . in an institution . . . and we believe him.'

Colby's ears perked up. He swung a quick glance at the cowering man, but he wasn't sure. He let her continue.

'He's been with us for two weeks and he's a kind, gentle soul who wouldn't do anybody harm. But he's scared, officer. He thinks you're going to lock him up and he's like a little child. So please be very, very careful . . . when you speak to him. We didn't know his whole story till we saw the news bulletin this evening and we want to do what's right. But we also want to know he's cared for . . . and we'd like to care for him ourselves, if it's possible . . . until this thing's resolved. He's our friend and we told him he wouldn't be hurt.' Her big eyes pleaded with Colby. 'Officer, this is Tony Buehl.'

Bull's eye, Colby thought. 'It's all right,' he assured Tony, who seemed to cringe more at the mention of his name. 'No one's going to hurt you.'

Tony relaxed a bit. 'You sure?' he asked timidly.

'Yes,' Colby answered. 'I promise.' He told the others, 'Would you folks come upstairs with me?' He saw further hesitancy on their faces. 'I promise you he won't be harmed.'

Escorting them to Homicide, Colby put them in Anunzio's office. 'I have to make a few phone calls,' he continued in the same upswing voice, 'then I'll come back and we'll talk.'

Colby made three calls. The first was to the Northeast Division to let them know

Tony Buehl had come home. The other two he made were prearranged instructions. Any breaks in either case or new developments, they were to call Lieutenant Lowenstein and Captain Anunzio. No matter what day, no matter what time.

* * *

When Asher walked in, it was 1:00 a.m. Only Colby and a few other detectives were pulling night shift duty. 'Where are they?' Asher asked.

Colby handed him his report. 'They're in Anunzio's office down the hall. The short brunette is Anna Belle Kolchinsky; the tall blonde, Claire Barrow-Montoya. The chunky guy is Santa Ana Montoya — '

'Santa Ana?' Ash cut in.

'I asked. Seems his parents named him after some Mexican president.'

'And revolutionary.'

Colby shook his head. 'This guy's cool. A live one left over from the sixties. Still into peace, love and brotherhood.'

Asher smiled. 'Nice sentiments. Go on.'

'The short guy with the straight brown hair is Sylvester 'Scrugs' Schrumphlinger.'

'Poor guy.'

'The poor guy has a record of arrest for possession of cocaine. Says he was set up.'

'Convicted?'

'No. Not enough evidence to make it stick. Judge at the preliminary hearing dropped the case.'

Asher shrugged and rubbed his eyes. 'Innocent until proven guilty.'

'That's what they all say.' Colby grinned.

'That's the law. What about this Thomas Murphy?'

'Tall muscular bald guy. Silent type. Wouldn't want to meet him in a dark alley, though.'

'And Tony Buehl?'

'The other little guy, partially bald. Scared silly. Thinks we're gonna call his brother.'

'Walter Buehl? Not if I can help it. The man's an asshole.'

Colby gave a quick laugh and smirked. 'Couldn't agree with you more, Lieutenant.'

'Lieutenant!' Another detective had picked up an incoming call. 'Police radio's on the line. They say another teenage boy was shot in the 15th District . . . about thirty minutes ago.'

'Alive?' Asher asked.

'So far. They took him to Frankford Hospital.'

'I'll take the call.' Asher moved to the desk, taking the phone. 'Hello, this is Lieutenant Asher Lowenstein. I'm the investigating officer on these cases. Could you give me the details, please, including the boy's condition?' The detective handed him a pen and clean note pad.

When he finished the call, Colby asked him, 'Where?'

'Wissinoming,' Asher said slowly, 'around Bridge and Torresdale in the Northeast.' Asher put his hand pensively to his chin, gazing into space.

'You okay?'

'Huh? Yeah, I'm just thinking.'

'Are you going to that hospital? I can help you out with Tony Buehl.'

'No, that's not necessary.' Asher let out a satisfied sigh and slumped into a nearby chair. He caught Colby's curiosity and explained. 'Our murderer shot at his would-be victim in the dark, Den. The boy, Peter Delaney, is listed in stable to good condition. The bullet impacted just below his left collarbone, then lodged in his shoulder. What's more, both he and his stepfather got a clear look at his assailant before the man fled. We've got ourselves two eyewitnesses.' Asher rose, paced a few steps, and grinned triumphantly. 'And maybe a third one. When the stepfather turned on the outside porch light, the killer was there with the wounded boy. He took a pot shot at the stepfather but he must've been nervous. The bullet whistled through the screen door and hit a mirror inside. When it shattered, the next-door neighbor switched on her porch light and came out to investigate. She only saw the man for an instant, but she saw him, just the same.'

Colby slowly, wonderingly, shook his head. 'Is some patron saint for cops blessing us tonight?'

'Looks like it. Dennis, what time did

Tony Buehl and his friends arrive here at Headquarters?'

'Around midnight.'

'The midnight hour,' Asher mused. 'There might be some magic in it after all. Sergeant Colby, call Captain Anunzio and give him the details on the Delaney boy. And tell him we've totally ruled out Tony Buehl as a suspect. Tell him I'll be calling Dr. Robbins and getting him down here as soon as possible. And lastly, tell him I have an idea I need to discuss with him first chance tomorrow morning. Got that?'

'I think I can handle it.'

'Good. I'll be in to see Tony Buehl as soon as I get Dr. Robbins apprised of this situation. Did you get them coffee or something?'

'Yep. They're taken care of.'

'Good.' Asher went to his desk, third down, got the file out on Tony Buehl and placed an emergency call to Dr. Robbins. Five minutes later, the good doctor rang him back. Asher filled him in on Tony's re-emergence. It was nearing 2:00 a.m. and Dr. Robbins promised to be there by three. Asher thanked him silently as well for his commitment to his patient, and hung up the phone.

He addressed Colby. 'Dennis . . . did you get through to the captain?'

'Yep. Says he'll be here at 8:00 a.m. and wants a complete briefing.'

'Good. A Dr. Alexander Robbins will be coming in here in about an hour. When he gets here, take him straight back to Anunzio's office. I'm going to see our runaway and his friends now.'

'You think you'll be all right with them?'

'I think so. If I have a problem, I'll call for backup.'

'Just playing it by the book, Ash. There's six of them and one of you. Just shout if you need me.'

'Will do,' he assured Colby, answering his concerned gaze, and both returned to their appointed tasks.

As he walked toward Anunzio's office, Asher pulled all thoughts from his mind, save one. Finally . . . he was going to meet the long-elusive Tony Buehl. Some more parts of the puzzle were falling into place and, if he played one last hunch right, he might link the last renegade piece. And it had to start with Tony Buehl and Dr. Robbins.

Could he do it legally, and would Dr. Robbins and the captain both agree to the gambit? Asher also knew his career might ride, precariously, on the outcome.

Asher walked in and saw the tight-knit little group turn their heads to look at him. He singled out Tony Buehl from Colby's description. 'Hello, Tony. I've been wanting to meet you.'

Tony looked at him innocently, surprised. 'You have?'

'Yes.' His voice was adamant but friendly.

'How come?' Tony waited.

'Because some people have been saying things about you that apparently aren't true.'

'I didn't do it.' He looked woebegone.

'Do what?'

'I ain't no killer. I ain't that man you showed on TV. Lotsa people look like that. Ain't that right, Scrugs?'

Scrugs patted his arm but didn't say anything.

'I know you're not a killer, Tony,' Asher assured him. 'But you did run away and we got to get that straightened out.' Asher spoke to them all. 'I'm Lieutenant Lowenstein, and if any of you are worried about the similarity between Tony and that sketch on TV, don't be. We have definite proof that he's not the man we're seeking.'

'How?' Claire asked.

'You folks gave him an alibi. When you brought him in here, another teen attack took place at the same time on the other side of this city.'

Annie Belle shot up from the chair she was sitting in. 'I knew it was important to bring him in tonight!'

'Huh?'

'You wouldn't understand it, Lieutenant. It was a feeling.'

'I'd understand a lot more than you think,' Asher said brusquely. But Annie only stared at him and he saw a smile spread on her face as she sat down.

'Officer . . . Lieutenant . . . another boy has been killed?'

Asher caught the tense concern in

Santa Ana Montoya's voice. 'No, he's not dead. We think he's going to pull through. You are not to repeat what I just said to you, Mr. Montoya.'

'Please . . . call me Santa.'

'It's not Christmas,' Asher muttered glumly, then waved it off with a nonchalant flick of his hand. 'All right. Santa.'

'It's my name, man.'

'Santa . . . would you and your troop listen very carefully? Has Tony mentioned a Dr. Robbins?' He caught a couple of nods. Tony stared at him intently but said nothing. He seemed to shrink again. 'Dr. Robbins is going to be here in about — ' he consulted his watch — 'forty minutes. He's very happy that you're safe, Tony.'

'My friends took good care of me.'

'I know. But, for a reason I can't explain yet, I don't want a lot of people to know you've been found.'

'You want me to hide some more.'

'Sort of. But I have to talk to Dr. Robbins first and another person.'

'Can I hide with my friends? I'll stay in the house. I won't go out.'

'I don't know yet, Tony.' He turned to Santa Ana. 'Are you the spokesman for this group?'

'We can all speak for ourselves. But I'm sort of the communal leader.'

'Commune? Are you people a commune?'

'Sort of. We're more like a family by choice. We take care of each other. And our lifestyle and beliefs are similar to some communes.'

'The last time I heard that word was in the late sixties.'

'There's a few communes left in Germantown. They've grown with the times, man, but for some of us, the dream didn't die.'

'I suppose that's admirable in its own way.' He stretched his neck wearily and went on. 'I want you people to promise me you won't leak Tony's reappearance if what I have in mind works out.'

Murphy gazed at him sharply. 'We won't. Won't do nothin' to hurt Tony. But what about you? What are your *plans?*'

'You have my word he'll be taken good care of. What's more, if Dr. Robbins agrees — and I can't see why he wouldn't — you'll know where he's at and can visit him.'

'Lieutenant!' Annie Belle stayed seated but her voice pitched high. 'If you need to keep Tony a secret, why can't he stay with us? We've already got a place for him.'

'I can't guarantee that until I talk with Dr. Robbins. He might not approve. And beyond that . . . I need my superior's permission. Without that, my involvement in this case will shortly be over.'

'You're tryin' to catch that killer, aren't you?' Santa asked.

Asher shot the heavy man an appraising gaze. 'We understand each other, Santa.'

Murphy spoke up. 'If the killer thinks Tony's been caught and the people think Tony's the killer, you're afraid he might go underground. Disappear on you.'

'Something like that,' Asher said.

A question slowly formed on Murphy's face. 'You really did think Tony was the killer.'

'I didn't. I didn't make a judgment on it either way. But Dr. Robbins assured me . . . strongly . . . that Tony was not the killer.'

Tony's dark brown eyes swelled up, accosting him with wonder. 'Dr. Robbins believed in me?'

'Yes, he did, Tony. All the way.'

A soft expression touched Tony's face. 'I like Dr. Robbins,' he murmured, lapsing into silence.

There was visible relief on all of their faces. Asher noted it, relaxing a bit for the first time in weeks, feeling the night going his way. 'Look, guys and girls, I'll get us more coffee. When Dr. Robbins gets here, I want you to fill him and me in on the whole story. How you met Tony, how you've been taking care of him. How Tony's been while living with you. Then I have to talk to Dr. Robbins alone. Afterwards, we'll come back and see where this all stands.'

'You got it, man,' Santa said. He glanced momentarily at the others and saw their approval. He yawned heavily. 'Now how's about that coffee?'

Asher allowed himself his own weary smile. 'Coming right up. I'll try not to keep you up too late.'

Santa smirked. 'I hope not, man. It's not Christmas.'

Asher's smile blew into a grin. 'Be right back.' He liked this man.

Dr. Robbins, he thought, *come through for me.*

Come through.

Then I'll try to scale Mount Anunzio. Convincing the captain would be the tough part.

★ ★ ★

Dr. Robbins shook hands with him. 'I think my wife is going to divorce me, Lieutenant Lowenstein. She says I earn enough as a shrink to keep proper office hours.' He was dressed casually in tan slacks and a polo shirt.

'Thank you for coming down here.'

'What else can I do? Tony's my patient and he ran away.'

'Is that the only reason?'

The doctor pursed his lips and raised his eyes. 'No.'

'You're a good doctor, doc.'

'Thank you. So where is my recalcitrant charge?'

'In a back office with his new family. They're going to fill both of us in on everything that's happened since Tony's disappearance. And you can ask Tony or them any questions you'd like. But afterwards I'd like to talk with you privately before we make a decision on where Tony goes tonight.'

'Tonight?' Dr. Robbins asked, his eyebrows arched.

'I'll explain later. Right now, I want you to see Tony and meet his friends.' He added in an aside, 'They're good people.'

'Apparently,' the doctor agreed. 'The wrong ones would've crucified him.'

9

'Do you have a couch, Lieutenant? I think my wife is right.'

Asher let out an exhausted chuckle. 'It's been a long day for me, too, Dr. Robbins. But now I want to discuss with you a reason for keeping Tony's recapture under wraps.'

'For what purpose, Lieutenant?'

'To catch the killer of those teenagers that's been plaguing this city.'

Dr. Robbins lifted his glasses to rub his eyes. 'Surely you know Tony's not involved.'

'Not personally. But possibly indirectly.'

'Indirectly, how? Something to do with his new friends?'

'No, not them. Doctor, you're a psychiatrist. How would you evaluate Walter Buehl?'

Asher watched the man's eyes grow wide and darken. 'Surely . . . ' Robbins fell into momentary silence. 'You don't think he's involved, do you?'

'Yes. But you haven't answered my question.'

Robbins's hand rose lightly to his chin. 'How would I evaluate him? You realize this is unofficial?'

'Of course.'

'A person just as deeply hurt as his brother Tony by their childhood tragedy. A person who hides that hurt well, but never learned to control it.'

'Control the anger?'

'Yes. It's in him, like a dormant volcano with all those gases bubbling at the core. But he directs it at Tony. Tony's his safety valve. He vents his anger on Tony by being a bastard to him all these years, keeping him locked up, using his position and authority to do so.'

'And when Tony escaped to freedom?'

'The man was a basket case,' was all Dr. Robbins could say.

'He may have been much more than that.'

'Lieutenant Lowenstein, do you have any *proof* of Walter Buehl's involvement?'

'I think so. And I think I'll have some more, enough to convince my captain to let me put a tail on him.'

'Then why put a tail on him? Why not just bring him in?' The doctor clearly wasn't convinced.

'Because I don't want this one to slip through our fingers, legally. The man has power, as well you've known. If he knows Tony's incarcerated again, that anger which I *think* has been vented on these modern teenagers because they remind him of Tony long ago, will get its original whipping boy back. And Walter Buehl will kick and claw his way out of an indictment at any legal cost.'

Robbins looked at him thoughtfully. 'You still haven't told me why you think Walter Buehl's your killer.'

Asher filled him in on the M.O. of the two murders, of the frustrating late night tail to the Northeast and the attack on Pete Delaney within the same neighborhood.

'You're right. It's all circumstantial,

unless that boy is willing to positively identify Walter Buehl as his attacker,' Dr. Robbins said. 'However, your psychiatric scenario is possible. Buehl could have enough deep-rooted anger, in my estimation, to have flipped when Tony disappeared. But I don't see what prolonging that instability would do.'

Asher leaned over, harsh and pleading. 'Buy us time. Let us collect more evidence.'

Dr. Robbins shook his head. 'It all sounds very scanty, Lieutenant.'

'Dr. Robbins, do you know what's going to happen if we pull him in and get him on the stand?'

'What?'

'He's going to play on Tony's resemblance to him. And on Tony's murder of his mother. He'll get other shrinks in to judge him homicidal. He'll put Tony on the stand.' Asher's diction became clipped, a rhythmic eulogy. 'Tony's next home *may* be a permanently barred cell.' Asher saw his words sink in. 'Maybe we'll win and maybe we'll lose. But I don't like maybes. Give me a little time to dig a deeper hole for Walter Buehl, or rule him out completely.'

Circles were deepening under Dr. Robbins's eyes. 'If he is your man . . . what if he kills again? Acting out this regressive fantasy because his whipping boy is gone?'

'You do believe it's possible, don't you?'

'Answer the question. It's important.'

'If we do go on this, we'll have a round-the-clock tail on Walter Buehl. Or we won't do it at all. I'll make that plain to my captain.'

Dr. Robbins sighed, worn out. 'Let's say, for now, I'm going with you on this. Temporarily,' he stressed, 'with a time limit on it as to how long you're going to look for tighter evidence or drop your suspicion of Walter Buehl. You still have to get your Captain's approval and I assume it will take at least a day. Where do you propose Tony stays in the interim, if I authorize this?'

Asher, bleary-eyed, silently prayed to whatever powers might be listening beyond those wielded by people like

Walter Buehl. 'Do you have any objection to his going home with his communal family? They've taken good care of him for two weeks and we'll know where he is at all times.'

He saw the doctor stiffen, then consider it. 'I'd have to speak to them. They'd have to be informed of his condition. There'd have to be an open line of communication, letting me know if there's a problem, letting me in to evaluate him. And my decision would have to carry final weight, on whether he stays or returns to the hospital.'

'Then you'll do it?'

'We'll try. To give you time. Just try to do me one favor.'

'What's that?'

'If it is Walter Buehl, get enough data to throw away the key without dragging Tony through the docks. He's made too good a scapegoat already.'

Asher slowly nodded.

Dr. Robbins rose stiffly. 'Now let's go talk to Tony and his newfound friends. It's almost dawn and I'm sure they would like to go home and sleep. Like me.'

★ ★ ★

Thursday, July 18th, 9:00 a.m.

'*No!*' The captain stood up abruptly. His eyes blazed, hot pincers of anger, on his lieutenant. He spread his thick hands hard against the polished desk top, so hard he felt it could crack the wood beneath. 'You trail a man to the same neighborhood and you expect me to call the man on it! Based on his vendetta with his brother, forty years old!'

'No, I don't expect you to do that. I expect you to hold your judgment until I get you more proof.' Asher's back was rigid, as if guarding his position in the precarious professional exchange.

Anunzio reseated himself slowly. 'By trailing him? Premature, Lieutenant. You've got to give me a lot more evidence before I authorize that on a man who's quite influential in our tri-state community.' He turned away from Asher, wondering if his chief detective had lost his mind.

'I intend to get you that evidence today or drop it.'

The captain turned to face him again. 'What evidence?'

'I've obtained a picture of Walter Buehl and I'm going to include it in a photo spread. Colby and I will be going over to Frankford Hospital. Peter Delaney's awake and capable of being questioned now. He's in good condition, of clear mind.'

Frank Anunzio felt his earlier thought of running out for coffee and a bagel would surely never sit quietly in his stomach now. How many times had he played with Buehl on that tennis court — a trim, controlled figure besting him two for one every time? Buehl, a closet nut? The thought frightened him, but he had been in the police business long enough to know there were no rules. *Be wrong*, he silently implored Asher, *or there goes another sweet illusion that I knew would come unglued one day. And it would have to be personal, the lesson getting kicked in my ass hard — not an isolated case, not a stranger whose strange face and class and money were isolated data; curious, interesting case data. Be wrong,* he prayed again. *Or be right, and I'll weep for the guy while I handcuff him. Shit. Why the ones who have everything?* He calmed himself, knowing he was running ahead of himself until Asher brought him that proof.

'I want positive I.D.,' he told Asher, who continued to sit tensely, bolt upright. 'Not a waver of doubt in that kid. Ready to sit on the witness stand, and I want that written on his signed statement. Without even the slightest hint of coercion!'

'If there's even the slightest doubt in Peter Delaney, I'll drop it. I know the procedural safeguards. Due process of law, sir.' Asher's confidence seemed to slack off. 'Even if it means giving up a lead I'm 99% sure of.'

'Ash,' Anunzio said, more gently. 'An I.D. will prove it out one way or the other. But we've got to play this one with kid gloves. The tiniest crack in your assumption, like false or mistaken I.D., will blow your case sky-high, too. So you've got to play this one straight on the line. I hope you're wrong.'

'I know you do, sir.'

'But this is your case, Lieutenant, and if *I'm* wrong . . . tough shit.' His voice was tinged with sadness. 'Go see your survivor. And report back to me on the double. By the way, you and Colby are pulling triple shifts as of this morning, aren't you?'

'Yes.'

'After we rule on this, I want you both to take the remainder of today off.'

'A couple of hours' sleep,' Asher agreed. 'If I'm right on this, I'd like to set up a plan of operation that prevents further violence as rapidly as possible.'

Anunzio didn't respond to his implication. 'Go to the hospital, Asher. I'll be here waiting, tackling this mountain of paperwork.' He reached over to the in-basket on his desk and lifted the first missive from its stack of wafer-thin letters and heavy reports. 'Dismissed.'

I'm sorry, Asher wanted to say. But he knew it was irrelevant and a waste of police time, unless he brought back proof. Facts were facts. Open a case because of solid evidence, or close it forever because the facts didn't cut it. Feelings, whether condolences or apologies, could be dealt with later. He lightly fingered a snapshot Dr. Robbins had pulled from his files: a picture of Tony, Dr. Robbins, and Walter Buehl taken by a hospital nurse during one of Buehl's reluctant, infrequent visits to see Tony. Buehl stood apart, coldly. Far enough apart for a clear blow-up.

★ ★ ★

Thursday, July 18th, 11:30 a.m.

The sandy-haired, hazel-eyed boy with the lanky but muscular build smiled up from his hospital bed at Asher Lowenstein and Dennis Colby. His upper left shoulder and chest were lightly bandaged and his arm was immobilized in a sling. 'Boy, this is just like on TV, Sarge,' he told Colby, youthful excitement heightening his voice.

'How do you feel, Pete?' Asher asked him.

'Fine, sir. They say I can go home in two days, if the break in my shoulder shows it's healing okay on the X-rays.'

'Good. Tell me, Peter, are you up to answering some questions, making a statement?'

'Sure.'

'Fine. Sergeant Colby here is going to get the basics down while I ask that pretty head nurse of yours to get us some coffee.'

Peter Delaney laughed. 'Could you ask her to get me some juice? I think they have grape.'

'I will. When I get back, I want you to look at some photographs and tell me if any of them is the man that attacked you. And if you're not certain, you tell me so. We don't want to arrest an innocent man.'

Pete shook his head as he spoke. 'Oh, I'll never forget that guy's face. I was staring at him after Joe turned on the porch light, after I was shot. I wasn't hurtin' bad, just stunned, you know? And starin' at that guy, like my eyes were glued to him, tryin' to figure out why he did that to me. Then, all of a sudden, I figured he had to be the Baby Boy Blue Killer, the guy in the sketch on TV, because of the fight my mom and I had takin' her home from the bar. It all happened quickly and I was gettin' faint from bein' shot and bein' scared outa my wits, thinking I had bit it, you know. But he was straight under that porch light and I'll never forget that face.' He gave his head one last shake for emphasis. 'Never.'

'Then you'll tell me if the photos do, or even slightly don't, look like the man who shot you.'

The boy nodded gravely. 'I won't say so unless I'm absolutely certain.'

'Good. Now I'm going for that coffee . . . and juice. You fill in Sergeant Colby here until I get back.'

Asher patted the hand of Pete Delaney's good arm as it rested on the wheeled hospital tray, and gave Colby the nod to begin. He went off to get the coffee and juice, leaving Colby to handle the primary details.

Ten minutes later, Asher returned and set the plastic tray down. 'Here, Pete.' He handed the boy the grape juice and he and Colby each took a cup of coffee. 'You finished?' he asked Colby.

'Yeah.' He handed Asher the large manila envelope containing the photo spread, a twelve-by-sixteen-inch piece of cardboard with eight photographs pasted onto it, and sipped the hot coffee gratefully.

Asher put his cup down and extracted the photo spread carefully. The pictures were arranged in two rows of four each. Each photo showed a man in late middle age, balding with slightly wavy hair of graying brown and dark eyes. Each face had a long hook nose, high cheekbones and high forehead, sparse eyebrows and small, almost delicate, lips. Eight narrow-faced men with slightly protruding ears. Eight faces with extremely similar features. 'Now, Pete I want you to look at each of these and make very sure before you identify any one of them as your attacker. We're going to go through them one by one.'

He pointed to the first photo, a sham

photo taken from police records to test the youth's power of observation.

'No,' Pete said, shaking his head.

Asher indicated the second picture, a similarly featured but older man, also a sham. Pete studied it carefully and shook his head again. 'It looks a little like him, but that's not him.'

Asher placed his finger on the third photo, a worried frown on his face. He waited for Pete's reaction; the boy studied it longer than the second. It was a blow-up of the earlier snapshot Dr. Robbins had sent to Asher with his initial letter to the Philadelphia Police, a blow-up of Tony Buehl's animated innocent face. *This one's for you, Captain*, Asher thought.

Pete continued to stare at the photograph. 'This really looks like him, but . . . ' He glanced up at Asher. 'I'm not certain. It might not be him, just someone who looks like him.' He laughed. 'This guy looks too nice to be that creep I saw.'

'Then you can't positively identify this photo as the man who attacked you.'

Pete took a deep troubled breath. 'No. I'm sorry.' He said it apologetically, apparently disappointed. 'You told me to be sure.'

'That's right. Absolutely sure. No guesses, not even near guesses. Let's go on to the next one.'

They moved through the fourth through seventh photos slowly. Pete Delaney checked each picture out and nixed each one.

Asher pinpointed the last photo in the spread, his finger coming slowly to rest on it.

Pete took the photo spread and held it loosely in his hand, his eyes lowering, fastening onto the last picture, the lines in his face hardening. 'Shit! That's the man.' He looked up at Asher; despite his sudden anger, a small spot of red appeared on his cheeks. 'Uh, sorry about cursing, Lieutenant.'

'Don't worry about it. That's the man?'

Pete stared again at the photograph. 'Yeah.'

'Are you certain enough about that that you could testify in court that this man was your attacker?'

Pete gave the photograph another scan. 'Christ, Yeah!'

'Okay, Pete. We're going to put that in your statement. Will you sign it? Be absolutely certain.'

Peter took one last look at the photograph. 'I'm certain. I'll sign it. I want to get that bastard.' The lines of his face remained rigid.

'So do we,' Asher assured him. 'We understand your stepfather and next door neighbor also got a clear look at the man. We want to talk to them also. But I want you to keep everything we've discussed here confidential, okay, Pete?'

'Sure thing, but why?'

'Because your attacker's still on the loose. We have to catch him.'

Peter shifted uncomfortably. 'Am I in danger? Because I identified him?'

'Yes,' Asher answered truthfully. 'Right now, the papers are reporting you survived the attack, and connecting it to the murders of the two other boys.' Asher had seen the morning edition.

Pete grimaced. 'There was a guy here earlier, asking to interview me. The head

214

nurse told him to leave.'

'When was this?'

'Uh, around nine to ten this morning. I remember I was watching Phil Donahue.'

Asher smiled slightly.

'Whatcha gonna do? About my being in danger?' Pete asked intensely.

'Provide you with police protection, like any important witness.'

Pete nodded. 'Oh, look. Here's Joe! I'll bet he can identify that guy, too. Will he get police protection, too?'

Stroke o' luck, Asher thought. 'Sure will,' he told him. He got up to greet the stepfather but Peter was quicker.

'Hey, Joe, this is Lieutenant Lowenstein and Sergeant Colby from the Philly police force. This here's my stepfather, Joseph Moscowicz.'

Asher shook the man's hand. 'This is opportune, Mr. Moscowicz. Your stepson just identified his attacker for us. We're hoping you can do the same. Do you think you could talk to us now?'

Joseph Moscowicz looked from Asher to Pete. 'Do you mind if I see Pete for a couple of minutes first? I took off from work this afternoon just to see him.'

'Not at all. I have to make a phone call to Headquarters anyway. Why don't we wait for you in the visitors' lounge?'

'Fine,' Joe agreed. He was a quiet man, up in years, with a look of trying to understand his world and not quite succeeding. 'Just want to talk to Pete for a little bit.'

Asher nodded, then motioned to Colby. 'See you later, Pete,' he waved.

'Hey, Lieutenant? When do I get my police guard?'

'As soon as I can hook it up. I'm calling my boss on it right now. Don't worry.'

'Protection?' Joseph Moscowicz betrayed vulnerable confusion, then worked visibly to pull himself together. 'I'll be in to talk to you in a moment, Lieutenant.'

'We'll be in the lounge,' Asher said.

* * *

Forty-five minutes later, arrangements were being made for police protection for both Peter Delaney and Joseph Moscowicz. Asher had two statements attesting to

216

positive identification of Walter Buehl as the attacker of Pete Delaney, and was on the way with Colby to get the statement of Marianne Wells, the Delaneys' next-door neighbor.

By 4:00 p.m. that afternoon, three witnesses had positively identified Walter Buehl as the assailant. Asher sat in the captain's office, across from a very glum Frank Anunzio, as they put together a plan and a timetable to tail Walter Buehl, to gather evidence to connect him to the two other murders as well.

Dr. Robbins had been filled in on the new development and agreed to give qualified professional testimony against Walter Buehl when the time came. He also agreed to give the Philadelphia Police Department all the time it needed, keeping Tony Buehl under wraps while they stalked his brother, Walt.

10

Asher lay exhausted on Tam's couch as sunset slowly melted into warm night. The fans in her apartment droned on in a lazy hum. He noted Tam had turned one refreshingly toward him. Its breeze caressed and cooled him.

Tam walked by, seeing his eyes were opened. 'You've been asleep for almost two hours,' she said softly. 'It's nine p.m.'

'Umm,' he answered. 'Feel like I could sleep another two or three.'

'Are you hungry?'

Ash lay still for a moment. 'Yes,' he said decisively.

'How's about a tuna sandwich loaded with salad?'

'Mmm! My favorite!' He started to rise, feeling every bone in his body creak.

Tam put her hands on his shoulders and gently pushed him prone. 'I'll call you when it's ready.' She planted a kiss on his forehead.

'Fresh-made,' he joked and shut his eyes again, giving in to drowsiness as crickets began their serenade outside the open windows beyond the sofa.

A short time later he felt a tender shake. He opened his eyes to Tam's reposeful smile. 'Do you think you can make it to the kitchen table?'

He smiled back at her. 'Not without one thing.'

'What's that?'

'This is not a come-on. It's something I really need.' A touch of melancholy swept through him. 'I really need it,' he repeated. 'I need you to kiss me.'

His tone left no doubt he did not mean his cheek or forehead.

'Please,' he whispered, and she lowered her face to his, her body bending against his. Their lips, closed lightly, met. Then emotion guided their arms: his around her back, one hand playing with her soft golden curls; hers, to rest against his chest, her hands clutching his shoulders, caressing and kneading. Their mouths parted slightly, only to act as prelude to deeper stronger kisses. Asher felt her heart beat strongly against his.

He had not expected this. He had made his request as a simple plea for human warmth with a pretty woman, a friend he felt love for and cared for. He had expected to share a quiet kiss, a moment's warm respite from the hardness of the world, and to hear light laughter as they broke apart and headed to the table. But the kiss lingered, sweet and urgent against the hushed sounds of the summer's night. Shadows deepened the apartment with their soft seductive air.

He tightened his grasp around her and felt her respond more strongly. Their mouths together tantalized. Again, he felt the furious pounding within her chest. Her warm flush grew more suffused, illuminating her face. *Tam*, he thought, ecstatic, purely amazed.

Tam slowly broke away from their embrace, her eyes misting with both shock and pleasure. 'Do you think . . . ' she began breathily, 'do you think you still want that tuna fish sandwich?'

Asher smiled hazily and regained his

own labored breath, tracing with his eye the curvature of her dimpled cheeks, the slight fullness of her lower lip. 'Yes,' he murmured back. 'I'm going to need my strength . . . when we get back to this later on tonight . . . if you're still willing, lady.'

'Asher . . . ' she began, her voice catching in her throat.

'Shh!' He stilled her, pressing his finger lightly against her lips, and rose into a sitting position. Taking her hand, he helped her up and they walked over to the table. He was seeing a new Tam and he wanted to see more of this new and wondrous woman he hadn't known was there. They sat at the table, still clutching hands.

'Where's David?' he asked.

'Staying overnight at a friend's. I told him I didn't want you disturbed.'

'The gods are beneficent.' He released her hand and picked up his sandwich. 'I want you for dessert,' he grinned.

Tam blushed.

'Are you still willing, angel?'

'I'm willing,' she whispered and looked

at him with eyes bright, pupils dilated.

From that moment, the night was theirs alone.

★ ★ ★

Friday, July 19th, 8:00 a.m.

Tam surveyed Asher's small apartment. 'This place could use a cleaning.'

Asher, fidgeting with his tie, freshly changed, ignored the innuendo. 'What time is it?'

'Just after eight. And you're avoiding my suggestion.'

He placed a light hand on her waist, pressuring her along. 'Come on, it's late. I want to get down to the office. I want to see how Dodd's doing with the first stage of the legwork.' John Dodd was a dour man in his forties, a loner by nature, and the best surveillance man in the Department. Anunzio had put him in charge of the three-man team assigned to shadow Walter Buehl. Asher found the man's cold, unemotional nature disconcerting as he and Colby filled Dodd in on Buehl. But listening to Dodd construct a comprehensive surveillance plan and discuss the best surveillance tactics had banished any personal dislike. The man was a pro; they listened avidly to him.

'I still don't see why you want me there,' Tam said.

'You're part of the team,' he reminded her. 'Unofficially, of course. At this point, it's up to us boys in the barracks to lay waste to Walter Buehl.'

'I don't see what good I can do at this point.'

'Send us good vibrations. Are you still worried about that dream you had?'

'That *repetitive* dream. Yes.'

'Psychological.'

'Right. Keep saying it, I might believe it.'

'It is,' he assured her as they left his apartment and moved toward his car. 'Thousands of mothers in this city are having like dreams every time their sons fight with them. And you and David don't fit the M.O. You never have loud furious arguments. So stop worrying.'

223

She pouted as he helped her into the car, then smiled up at him and shook her head. 'I hope you're right.'

'Worry wart,' he said. He closed the door, walked to the other side and got in.

She turned to him. 'Why do you want me there?'

He put the key in the ignition but didn't turn it. 'To continue to give your impressions. Your psychic sketch was right on target, way before we had hard proof linking Walter Buehl. You've been helpful in many other ways. I want you around whenever you can be, to soak up the atmosphere, to let me know if you pick up anything. And aside from that, I need your assurance. I need someone to tell me we're going to get the bad guy. Look into your crystal ball and tell me if you see justice on the horizon.'

'I'm not the only one who's worried.'

'No,' he admitted, starting the car. He pulled out and headed toward Cottman Avenue. 'Well, what do you see?'

'Justice.'

'Strong impression?' he asked.

'Blind faith,' she answered. She leaned

forward to switch on the car radio. EAZY-101 flooded the interior with soft contemporary music.

He reached over and squeezed the soft flesh of her upper arm gently. 'That's good enough,' he told her.

They drove on in silence, letting the music soothe them, a sedative against the new uncertain day ahead of them.

*　*　*

They were ushered into Anunzio's office the moment they arrived. Dodd was sitting in a chair opposite the captain. He greeted Asher and appraised Tam quizzically.

The captain rose and waved in her direction. 'Tam Westington, John Dodd.' His hand swung back to Dodd, and he reseated himself. 'Tam is a psychic investigator who's recently begun working with us.'

Tam took in the thin swarthy man with pitch-black hair and moustache, and skin the color of burnished walnut. She picked up a taut line of tension following

Anunzio's introduction.

Dodd's eyebrows lifted skeptically. 'A psychic. Is she any good? Track record?' He continued to stare coldly at Tam.

She fixed him with an equally forceful stare. Rather than close himself out, the man had opened up a keyhole with his honesty. She picked up a direct memory, so strong she was absolutely certain of it. 'Your mother always said you were skeptical. About God and spiritual things,' she added.

Dodd seemed taken aback but immediately regained his control. 'An easily-inferred impression, Ms. Westington.'

'Yes, and an equally true one.' She hesitated then continued. 'Also true that you were seven years old when you refused to go to church because you couldn't see God and didn't believe He existed. I believe it cost you a great deal of punishment.'

Dodd's eyes widened but he remained absolutely motionless. 'Eight,' he corrected. 'I don't know who or what you are but you're good. Do you see anything else?' It was a challenge.

'Only that with certainty. I don't intend to play it further with guessing games.'

'Try me.'

Tam stood rigidly, then responded in a low, modulated voice. 'First, you know who I am, and what I am is a person like yourself with talents you haven't developed yet, perhaps have no knowledge of having. Whether you do or don't is not my concern. Having someone set me outside the spectrum of humanity is my concern and I won't stand for it.'

Dodd inclined his head, eyelids lowered halfway, in a quiet nod of acquiescence. Then his gaze lifted to meet hers once more, respect mingling with reserved judgment. 'Is she on our side?' he asked Asher.

Asher only smiled.

'You never went back to church,' Tam said.

'That's a definite?' Dodd asked her.

'Oh, yes. At least, not for religious purposes.'

There was a visible relaxing of Dodd's stance. His tone was conversational. 'I saw too much pain and misery. And the dead never came back to talk.'

Tam knew there was much more but didn't probe, within herself or him. She simply said, 'I'm not here to decide your reality for you. And neither would I want to. It's your choice.'

'And neither would I assume to make yours,' Dodd said, a smile creeping lopsidedly onto a corner of his thin lips.

Tam moved over to him and held out her hand. It was a deliberate act. She sensed his willingness to trust her, at least for what she was worth.

Dodd slowly took her hand, shook it twice firmly and inclined his head in that decisive nod he seemed to own.

'Tam described Buehl before we had a lead on him,' the captain said quietly.

John Dodd greeted her again with that quirky half-smile. 'Remarkable lady.' Then he addressed his superior. 'Shall we get down to business?'

'Let's have your report.'

Dodd took out a cigarette, lit it, and took a drag. 'I pulled the initial surveillance on Walter Buehl from 7:00 p.m. last night to 8:00 a.m. this morning. Buehl arrived home from work, freshened up and went out again. I trailed him to a favorite watering hole in Society Hill, *The Knave of Hearts*. Respectable looking joint, nice clientele. He appeared to be a regular. The bartender knew his name.' He reached down to his briefcase on the floor beside his chair, opened it, and handed Anunzio a typed report. 'I hung around at the end of the bar and listened. Buehl did a lot of talking about the Delaney boy and how he was lucky to escape the 'maniac.' The bartender played right up to his rap, seemed to have heard it before. Then Buehl got confidential with the barman, told him he was working with the police because he knew who the killer was. Didn't mention his brother by name, though. The important thing was his insistence that the killer would strike again in a few days if the cops didn't find the man he knew was the killer. When the barkeep asked him how he knew, Buehl got tense and mumbled something too low for me to make out. I caught the word 'missing.' The bartender was obviously impressed and kept probing him for extra details.

Buehl said the data was secret, got flustered and made some excuse to leave. He walked around south Philly for a half hour, seemingly searching for something or someone, and would stop at intervals and look back. I had to be careful trailing him. At first I thought he was on to my tail, but that proved incorrect. At one point, I walked right by him and stopped at a nearby bus stop. He walked past me, completely preoccupied. He got back to his car and drove home. I kept an eye on him till 8:00 a.m. when Colby relieved me. I filled Colby in on his habit of glancing back on these constitutionals of his. Nothing further to report.'

Anunzio nodded. 'He spoke of Delaney while in the bar?'

'Can I give you an impression?' Dodd's hand cupped his chin, elbow on the chair's arm.

'Go on.'

'This man has no memory of his attack on Delaney.'

'How sure is your impression?' Asher asked him.

Dodd swung his gaze to Asher. 'He

absolutely believes another man did it. And he's furious with the man who did. My impression.'

'Did he mention the other two murders?' Anunzio asked him.

'Briefly. While he mentioned Delaney. Come to think of it . . . ' Dodd paused.

'What?' Anunzio asked.

Dodd narrowed his eyes, remembering. 'He said even though the Delaney kid was no good, just like the other two, at least he didn't die. Then he ripped into some dialogue about Delaney's being lucky the killer didn't finish him off.'

Asher looked at Tam, then spoke to the surveillance man. 'Paul Mandel kept repeating those words, *no good,* after he was shot. And Walter Buehl flung them at his brother, Tony, forty years ago, after Tony stabbed their mother. It's listed in his medical records on a brown and aging document. The physicians who evaluated Tony at that time insisted on knowing Walter Buehl's reaction and how it possibly affected Tony's condition.'

'Do we have a copy of that document?' Anunzio asked him.

'It's in the file.'

'Get it.'

Asher left the room, retrieved both files on the Buehl brothers and brought them back to Anunzio's office. He riffled through one file. 'Here it is.' He read: 'Sergeant Keller reported the younger brother, Walter Buehl, to be repeating, 'You're no good. You're no good. You're a no-good kid and you oughta be dead.' As both children were led to the squad car, Walter Buehl continued to shout to Anthony Buehl, 'You oughta be dead.'' Asher put the report slowly back in the file. The paperwork rustled in the silence.

The phone on Anunzio's desk rang. He answered it curtly, putting it on speakerphone. 'Yes?'

'This is Officer Wyker in the lobby, sir,' a woman's voice told him. 'There is a Walter Buehl here asking to see you.'

The silence grew tense, expectant.

'Tell him I'll be with him in five minutes, Officer Wyker.'

'Will do, sir.' She clicked off.

Anunzio stared at the others. 'Well?'

'Send him in,' Dodd said dryly.

'You'd chance being here?'

'He already knows Asher's and Colby's faces. And if the tactics I've shown them are working, they could have a drink with him — he wouldn't know a shadow if he tripped over it. Other than to dismiss it as coincidence. And — ' he paused, 'if my previous impression was right, this should prove very interesting.'

Anunzio seemed relieved, not having to face it alone. 'Let him do the talking. Don't offer anything but ordinary comment.' Then he muttered to himself, 'This could blow it.' He rang the lobby desk back. 'Officer Wyker, have someone escort Walter Buehl to my office. And hold my calls until he leaves. No exceptions.'

'Yes, sir.'

They waited, dense tension filling the room.

Asher suddenly remembered the files. 'Captain,' he said, lifting them.

Anunzio took them and threw them in a file drawer. A knock sounded on the door. 'Come in.'

Walter Buehl entered and noted the

crowd. 'Perhaps I came at a bad time.'

'No, no, Walter. Sit down.' He indicated the empty chair beside Dodd. 'We were just wrapping up some business.'

Buehl sat down in the chair, looking uncomfortable.

'What brings you here, Walter?'

'Concern, as usual. I'm sure you're aware of that attack on that young boy in Wissinoming. The papers said he might be able to identify his attacker. If Tony could be found and brought to this boy, I'm sure we could end this horror right now.'

'Your brother . . . Tony?' Anunzio slowly asked.

'Yes. I can't impress upon you how certain I am he is the maniac.'

'Captain,' Asher interposed, 'perhaps I can fill Mr. Buehl in, being I'm heading that investigation.'

'By all means.' The captain made a sweeping gesture, palm up, giving Asher the floor. A bit too eager and tense, but Buehl seemed not to notice as Asher positioned himself to face him.

'We're continuing our general radio

messages on your brother, Mr. Buehl, and one of our officers believes he may have sighted him down on Front Street, near the waterfront. We're having patrols watch that area now. We also believe some unsuspecting person or persons may be sheltering him. I assure you, as soon as he's found, we'll make every effort to see if he is involved or not.'

'He is,' Walter Buehl said somberly.

'We hear what you're saying, Mr. Buehl,' Asher responded just as gravely.

'Lieutenant Lowenstein, you must increase patrols in that neighborhood. It's almost a certainty he might attack again, perhaps kill again.' Buehl looked at him, eyes glazed, pupils dilated with unrestrained emotion. He beseeched Frank Anunzio, his voice crescendoing upward by degrees. 'You understand, don't you, Frank? You see the importance of this, don't you?'

Anunzio's eyes were filled with sadness. He took a deep breath. 'Yes. Don't you worry, Walter. Everything will be fine.' He said it soothingly. Buehl calmed down.

'Then I have your word you'll keep

these efforts going?' He addressed his concern to Asher.

'You have my word,' Asher told him solemnly.

Buehl rose. 'Then I'll leave you fine gentlemen to conduct your investigation.'

He offered first Asher his hand, then Anunzio. They both shook it.

'Take it easy, Walter.' Anunzio smiled.

Buehl smiled woodenly back, nodded a stiff farewell to Tam and John Dodd and moved to the door. 'Call me at the slightest development,' he said.

'We will,' Asher said in a firm tone. Buehl let himself out.

Silence redescended in the room. A few minutes later, the phone rang again. Anunzio answered it. 'Yes.'

'Sergeant Colby's reporting in, sir. I have him on hold. He wants to know if — quote — everything's all right and should he continue Operation Blue?'

'Affirmative to both questions. Tell him to continue.'

'Yes, sir.'

Anunzio sat back in his chair, looking leveled.

'He doesn't know he's doing it,' Tam said quietly.

Asher stared at them morosely. 'That's a sick man.'

'Loco.' Dodd sucked in his cheeks in an already thin face and smacked his lips in consternation. 'And dangerous.'

★ ★ ★

Saturday, July 20th, 2:00 p.m.

Asher helped Tam out of the car; David let himself out of the back seat.

'Are you sure you don't mind my dropping you off in town later? I have to go on duty at four, but if you want, we can cut this visit short, early on. I could drive you home.' Asher took her hand and the threesome started up Coulter Street to No. 837.

'No, it's okay. I really have to get this sprouting kid some new summer jeans and tops.' She looked at David with motherly disgust; he had cut off the sleeves on the T-shirt she had given him a month ago. He wore it now bare-armed, the shirt a bit ragged where he had performed its mutilation with the scissors.

David grinned at her. 'It's the style, Mom. Besides, it's cooler.'

Right, Tam thought. 'Well, I'm getting you some sleeveless polos. I don't intend to buy things to see them torn up.'

'Great. See if they have those fishnet tops!'

Tam blanched, but said nothing further. She made a mental note to try to avoid stores with fishnet tops. Teenage fashion. One of life's losing battles.

They reached No. 837 and rang the bell. A large figure loomed behind the screen door and she saw David grin at his size. It had to be Santa Ana. Asher had filled her in on Tony and his new family of friends.

'My man!' Santa greeted Ash effusively. 'Come on in. Come on in!' He opened the screen door and ushered them inside.

'These are my friends, Tam Westington and her son David,' Asher said. 'Tam does occasional work with us at the Philadelphia Police Department. She's a psychic.'

'Far out,' Santa said, impressed. 'Annie Belle would be interested in that.'

'Annie Belle's their resident psychic,' Asher reminded her.

Tam looked around. She liked the place. It had a good feel to it. She saw a straggly-looking fellow descending the stairs to the right of Santa Ana. He smiled at Asher and suddenly shouted up the stairs.

'Hey, you guys, Lieutenant Lowenstein is here! Hey, Tony, Lieutenant Lowenstein came here to see you!'

Suddenly the house filled with movement and noise. Tam, David, and Asher were surrounded, inundated, with smiling figures and eager faces. Warmth. So much warmth. Tam smiled back at the remarkable warmth encircling them.

Claire brought out the coffee and two plates piled high with assorted donuts. David reached over, quickly claiming the toasted coconut. 'David, don't grab,' Tam chided him.

'Oh, no, it's all right. Guests first,' Claire said, walking around the table, pouring the coffee into mugs. She

239

finished pouring, placed the large metal pot on a hot plate, and sat down. 'Tony's been looking forward to this all day.'

'Well, Tam and David wanted to meet him, too, and the rest of you.' Asher fished out a glazed donut and offered the plate to Tony. Tony scanned the plate and chose the powdered jelly.

'Tam, how long have you been psychic?' Annie Belle asked.

'Oh, since I was a teenager, maybe earlier and not aware of it. I was always shy about it, a little bit afraid of it in the beginning.'

'I was like that, too. But my parents said it was a gift from God and I should always treat it sacredly.'

'Oh, I couldn't talk about it at all to my parents. They thought I was imagining things,' Tam confided, amazed at the unhampered ease she felt with these people. 'Even now, my father doesn't believe in it and says I'm kooky. My mother, well, she believes there's something, that these things are possible . . . but she doesn't make a judgment.'

'Lost people,' Annie Belle intoned.

240

'Lost and ignorant of the vast power of the human mind and soul. Of the universe.'

'Perhaps they don't need to know it,' Tam suggested. 'And they're not meant to. Perhaps they have other things to attend to in their lives, other things that call to them.'

'Wise,' Annie Belle softly complimented her. 'Perhaps I was a bit harsh.'

'A bit,' Tam agreed amicably, her years of living with those uninitiated in psychic matters — both the curious dissenters and the hard skeptics — giving her more tolerance. 'It's fear of the unknown that mostly turns people away from exploring the psychic world. Or, as I've said, they have no need. If one doesn't need, one doesn't seek. When it's time for them to do so, or a need arises for it in their lives, then they open up their vista.'

Annie Belle nodded gravely, impressed. 'Where do your talents lie in the psychic world?'

'Oh, they're scattered. I'm a sensitive, an empath. I can pick up other people's feelings when they're projecting them strongly — even when they won't admit verbally to them. I have some ability in telepathy and psychometry. I have healing ability and I believe I have mediumistic abilities, although I'm very careful and cautious about dealing with that.'

'The spirit world is dangerous to an inexperienced person,' Annie Belle agreed.

'Not if you have friends there,' Tam said, and immediately blushed. She had never told Asher about that portion of her talent. Even David, usually so supportive, drew his line there and looked at her in askance.

'Yeah, my mother talks to ghosts,' David said pleasantly, and he shrugged his shoulders as if to say it was beyond his ken. 'Silently, of course. She doesn't talk out loud . . . usually. Can I have another donut, please?'

'Go ahead, help yourself,' Claire said.

Tam looked around, gauging the reaction to David's words. It was a part of her reality she could never deny, but so controversial, she often treated it as personal and private. When she did discuss it, she considered such communication thin ice

— one wrong word capable of truly break-ing it, leaving only cold murky water, drowning understanding.

She felt a tension to her left, emanating from Asher. She wanted to put her hand on his arm, and say: *I never told you because* . . . But the thought stayed frozen, hidden, as she was fearful of losing him.

Annie Belle picked up the thread of conversation deftly. 'The spirit world is a very valid reality,' she said, to everyone in general. 'But there are limitations to the communication between this spiritual world and our mortal one. Because of this, most people find it hard to believe how closely the two worlds are connected. They usually have to have some personal experience or have some friend whose sanity they trust without question tell them of a personal experience, before they'll open up to some belief. Still, it's remarkable in this scientific age: there are so many things we can't see or feel that science admits to being real, but the question of the spiritual still comes under fire.' She knocked on the table with her knuckles. 'But not everything that's real is solid and visible.'

Tam felt she couldn't have said it better. She watched Asher's open surprise as he reassessed the tiny brunette woman. But she still felt remaining tension in him, lessened though it was.

'I've just never seen a ghost,' Asher said lamely.

'Exactly,' Santa Ana shot in. 'Maybe, like your lady says, you never had the need to. You just haven't opened up to that portion of reality.'

Scruggs, across from Tam, nodded in agreement.

'He's got other things to deal with,' Murphy said, his voice centered on the here-and-now. 'I can dig it. I never seen no ghost either. But my lady here says they're called *entities* and they think and feel and live just like we do. She says the good ones don't go haunting people. But I ain't psychic so I never saw no ghost.' He spread his large hand in a slight shrug. 'But I believe Annie. Cause I trust her. She's proved out the other stuff.'

The group murmured agreement of

Annie Belle's credentials. She smiled secretly at Tam, who picked up a sudden picture of Asher and the words, *he'll be fine*. Tam stared back at her, thankful, but flustered. She sensed a relaxation in Asher, but said nothing, staying out of it while she was ahead.

'Listen, guys and gals,' Asher said, checking his watch, 'I hate to break this up, but it's three thirty and I go on duty at four. I'm afraid we have to leave.'

'Oh? But you've only just gotten here,' Claire said. 'Maybe Tam and David would like to stay. We could drive them home.'

'Well, Ash was going to drop David and me off downtown. I have some shopping to do.'

Annie Belle put her hand to her chin, studying the situation. 'Why don't we girls go shopping? Claire can drive us downtown. Then the lieutenant won't be late.'

'Well, I don't know.'

'Can I go, too?' Tony asked, hopeful.

Asher looked sternly at him. 'No, Tony.'

'Please. I won't be no trouble!'

'He hasn't been out for three days,' Claire ventured.

Tam considered, then said slowly, 'I can go with them. If there's trouble, I'll call Headquarters right away to notify you.'

Asher deliberated. 'You're just going shopping.' He eyed Claire and Annie Belle. 'No side ventures now. I don't want him out in the open too long.'

'We'll bring him right back,' Claire promised.

'Lieutenant Lowenstein,' Scrugs said warily, 'if you think it's dangerous for Tony . . .'

'I'll be good!' Tony cut in breathlessly. 'Can't I just be in the sunshine a little bit? In the car?'

Asher gnawed his lower lip, then made a decision. 'Can one of you men go with them?'

'I'll go,' Murphy said. 'No one's gonna mess with me.'

'I believe it.' Asher smirked. 'Okay. But only for an hour or two, no more. And no gallivanting around!'

'I'll see to it that they don't,' Tam said. 'I don't sense anything dangerous.'

Asher locked his eyes deeply with hers. 'You call me if you need me,' he told her firmly. He gave her a small sensual kiss on the lips that invited a later rendezvous. 'I've got to go. Take good care of this lady and her son. They're very special to me.' He rose, patted Tony's shoulder and ruffled David's hair.

'Hey, watch the hair,' the boy protested. 'It took me long enough to get it combed right!'

'Teenagers,' Scrugs laughed, and the others joined in as they walked Asher to the door.

'Call me tonight when you get home,' Tam said, adding, 'even if it's late.'

'Will do,' he answered, his fingers brushing her cheek. He smiled at the others and left, the lateness of the hour showing in his gait as he hurried down the street.

'Well,' Claire said, 'if we want to get to those stores before they close, we'd better clean up and get going.'

'I'll clean up, honey,' Santa offered.

'You go ahead. Murphy, take good care of them.'

'I'll only be a second.' Claire smiled. 'Let me get my purse.'

11

The hot summer air was dispersed as breezes swept through the open windows of the station wagon. 'It feels so good to be out in the sunshine,' Tony said, enjoying the drive. He sat between Murphy and Annie Belle in the back as they sped along the expressway into Center City.

'When all this is over, you can get out more,' Tam consoled him.

'You know, Mom,' David said, sitting beside her in the front with Claire, gazing out the window. 'I don't see what all the fuss is about Tony.' He turned to speak to Tony. 'You seem okay to me.'

'Well, that's between Tony and his doctor,' Tam told him.

'You know, Tam,' Claire said, 'maybe you can help us to convince Dr. Robbins to let Tony stay with us . . . after this is over.'

'I'll mention it to Asher. I understand

they do have foster-home-type set-ups. Maybe they can do that for Tony and have a case worker come out.'

'I hope they can,' Annie Belle said intensely, and Tam could hear the mothering in her voice. *Strange*, Tam thought. *Strong and beautiful, these people*.

'He's like a brother now,' Murphy said.

Tony said nothing, but as Tam swung a glance around, she caught the sheepish smile plastered on his face. 'I'll do what I can,' she told them.

'I'll vouch for Tony!' David assured them. He saw his mother roll her eyes upward.

Murphy laughed. 'Well, it can't hurt,' he said.

They emerged from Strawbridge & Clothier, laden with shopping bags.

'Charge card heaven,' Tam said. 'How I survive when David needs new clothes!'

'Yeah, charging is fun,' Claire said, hefting her own purchases up to a more comfortable carrying position. 'It's so hot, you know what I think we should do?' She waited until they all looked at her expectantly. 'Go have a drink on the *Moshulu*.'

'Oh, I don't know about that,' Tam protested, remembering the false report Asher had fed to Walter Buehl.

'Of course, David and Tony will have to stick to non-alcoholic fare.' She misread Tam's concern.

'You're worried,' Annie Belle told Tam. 'Don't be. I sense no danger. Search within yourself.'

Tam did. Sunshine, pleasantry, good vibrations were all that presented to her probe. 'You're right,' she agreed. 'But just one drink. Then we go.'

'You're on, boss lady.' Murphy smiled amiably.

'Oh, good,' David said, and Tam remembered his fascination with ships.

'David loves boating and ships,' she told them. 'He wants to join the Navy when he's older.' She turned to Annie Belle as they headed to the wagon. 'You know, I had a bad dream about the *Moshulu* two weeks ago. Asher said it was psychological. David was in it.' She shuddered at the memory.

251

'I pick up your concern,' Annie said. 'But I don't see anything that'll hurt us.'

'Maybe it was psychological,' Tam conceded. 'Okay. One drink.'

★   ★   ★

'Let's go up on the upper deck,' Annie said. 'We can watch the boats.'

The *Moshulu*, a famed floating restaurant along Penn's Landing, held two dining and lounging decks. The lower deck held a restaurant and enclosed lounge that Asher had taken Tam to a year ago for cocktails. She had loved sipping their drinks while looking out the window at the sparkling water reflecting the night lights on both the Philadelphia and Camden, New Jersey sides of the Delaware. The boat had rocked gently as she and Ash relaxed in the comfortable upholstered lounge chairs, the little lounge table between them and the candle atop it moving with the motion of the ship. So much so that Tam had pushed the candle back to the center of the table with a cautious air.

Now she smiled toward that lounge area, remembering that night and the sleepy lulling feeling of that evening. Claire tugged her arm, bringing her out of her reverie. 'Come on, Tam. This way.' She led them to an upper deck, which also housed a bar. On one wall were nautical pictures. David drew toward them, walking away from his mother and the others.

'Hey, Mom, check out these pictures!'

Tam turned to see David, still halfway across the room, head bobbing from one photograph to another, engrossed in them. A vague sense of unease crept up on her.

'Come on, David. Let's stay together.' Her worry was mounting; as long as they stuck together, it couldn't be like the dream. She and David had been alone in the dream, until Asher came.

And Asher was now on duty, trailing Walter Buehl. How ridiculous were her worries . . . motherly worries. 'Come on, David!'

'Aw, Mom!'

'Come on!'

He sighed and joined the others and together they found a table on the open air deck outside. It provided a full vista of the Delaware River. Sun glinted brightly on the water. A speedboat jaunted by, cascading waves outward in its wake. A goodly number of other people relaxed at tables on the deck, enjoying the serene gentle swells that rocked the restaurant ship like a cradle. There again, the dream differed. The other tables had been empty.

Tam felt her tightened muscles loosen, leaning back in the chair, giving in to the soothing rhythmic swaying of the *Moshulu*. A waitress came over to take their order.

'Gin and tonic,' Claire said.

'A glass of burgundy,' Annie Belle ordered.

The waitress turned to Murphy.

'A bottle of Schmidts.'

Then Tony.

'Do you have lemonade?'

The waitress smiled. 'No. Coke, Ginger Ale, apple juice and orange juice.'

'Orange juice,' Tony said.

'I'll have the same,' David told her.

The waitress turned to Tam.

'Scotch and soda,' she said.

The girl hurried away to fill their order.

'Boy, this is fun,' David said, watching each boat that cruised by. 'Look at that. That's a forty-footer.'

'Yeah,' Tony said. 'It's fun.' He looked uncomfortable. 'Murphy? I have to go to the bathroom.'

'Okay, come on. I'll take you there.' He turned to Annie Belle. 'Don't drink my beer, kiddo.'

'Right!' She made a sour face.

Murphy steered Tony away to the restrooms below. Tam, Annie Belle and Claire chatted lightly as the drinks were served.

'They went to the little boys' room,' Claire joked as the waitress eyed the two empty seats.

'Oh,' the girl laughed and distributed the round.

'Tam.' Annie Belle sipped her wine. 'You and Asher are going together?'

'Sort of. It's just recent.'

'Mmnn. He's cute.'

'Yeah,' Claire agreed, a conspiratorial girlish grin stretching her face.

A tad hint of a blush she could feel rising hit Tam's cheeks. She smiled at her new friends impishly. 'I think he's sorta *gorgeous*,' she confided, the memory of his kisses bringing back their pleasure two nights ago.

'I think you're in love,' Annie Belle laughed. 'It's such a nice feeling.'

Claire nodded wistfully.

'Mom, can I go look at the ship?' David asked. 'I mean . . . you women are talking girl talk . . . can I please?'

Tam hesitated, noting how sunset had arrived — pinks, mauves and lavenders mixing with the remaining blue of the sky and highlighted by bright streaks of yellowed gold. There'd been no sunset in the dream. 'Don't go far away,' she ordered.

'I'll just be on the deck below.'

Tam knew he meant the intermediate deck between the two restaurant deck levels, the iron-decked port and stern of the *Moshulu*. She watched him scamper past the tables and climb down the ladder to the deck, portside. Once he cleared the ladder, from where Tam sat on the lounge deck, David was out of her view. But her gaze stayed locked in that direction; fear rose within her despite her efforts to clamp it. *It was just a dream*, she told herself.

She felt a small hand on hers. Annie's hand. 'Don't *worry*,' she said.

Tam shook her head as if to shake away the apprehension. But a chill seared through her as she looked up and saw Asher emerge hastily through the doorway of the upper deck. He strode over to her, his anger evident. 'What are you doing here?' His tone, though quiet, reproached her sharply. 'You said you were going straight home.'

'There's no danger here,' Annie explained.

Asher sighed so heavily it heaved his shoulders. 'Ladies, Murphy took Tony to the public restroom outside because the *Moshulu*'s was overcrowded. Walter Buehl was outside and saw them. Luckily, he lost them in the crowd, and I could call for backup. They're waiting for you in the parking lot with Sergeant Colby. You ladies are going to leave this place right now.' He pulled out his wallet as he spoke and placed a twenty-dollar bill under Murphy's untouched glass of beer. 'Tam, go get David, and be quick about it. I want you out of here and straight home.'

'Right away,' Tam said. She moved through the crowd to the ladder, climbing gingerly down to the unadorned intermediate deck. David stood at its far end, leaning over the railing, studying something intently on the port bow.

'David, come on. We have to go,' she called, moving toward him. His head lifted at the sound of her voice. He wore his disappointment plainly. 'Aw, Mom!'

'David, there's danger here. We have to go.'

'What danger?'

'Asher's here. They spotted Walter Buehl on Penn's Landing and they think he's seen Tony.'

'So if Asher's here, he'll protect us,' David argued.

'*I said let's go!*'

She grabbed his arm to guide him

forcibly along. His face registered embarrassment and shock. It was something she hadn't done to him in years.

'Jesus Christ, Mom! I can walk on my own speed!' He pulled his arm back abruptly as he spoke, tightening his muscles, breaking her hold on it. His fist was clenched.

'You're no good!'

The voice, tinged with disgust, sounded directly behind them.

David's eyes went huge. His angry self-assurance just minutes ago drained out of him now. He stared past her, pale with terror.

Tam slowly turned to face Walter Buehl.

He wielded a small pistol with what appeared to be a silencer attached to it. He aimed it at them. 'I can't let you hurt Mom, Tony. I can't let you hurt her anymore.'

He lifted the gun an inch.

Oh, God, Tam thought. She assessed her predicament quickly. 'I'm not hurt, Walter,' she said. 'I'm not hurt. You see?' Tam pulled all the soothing resonance she could muster into her voice. She wished she could link eyes with him — the right gaze could control him — but her own gaze kept straying to that gun, knowing any minute . . .

'It's all right, Walter. I'm all right. Don't hurt the boy!'

Buehl's face clouded over. He appeared dazed. 'You're not Mom,' he muttered, his confused state evident.

Tam watched Asher and Dodd climbing slowly down the ladder, seeming miles away from the confrontation she faced. 'Stay directly behind me, David,' she said tonelessly. Buehl continued to point his gun their way, but uncertainty seemed to stay his hand. Behind them, Asher and Dodd advanced onto the deck, guns drawn also. But Tam knew they wouldn't shoot, not while she and David were in the line of fire. Unless they were close enough for a clean shot.

The ship pitched from a swell from a passing boat. Beyond them, a commotion sounded from the upper deck as patrons took notice of the drama on the forward bow. Buehl turned to see Asher and Dodd closing in, guns pointed.

'Freeze, Buehl!' Asher shouted.

Tam reached behind slowly with her hand, fingers open and insistent. She felt David grasp it. She sidled them, inching minutely but steadily to the left, out of the line of fire.

The ship suddenly pitched, harder this time, nearly throwing them onto its deck, their coordination marred by fear. A muted shot was heard, barely audible, as the ship settled back and screams sounded on the deck above. Tam and David hit the deck instinctively, Tam praying. More commotion and screams sounded from the restaurant. Tam lifted her head to see Asher grabbing his shoulder. Walter Buehl, in flight, collided with John Dodd as the ship heaved again and Dodd raced to intercept Buehl and cut off his escape. She watched the impact knock Dodd onto the deck, gun arm held aloft, his other arm flailing to break his fall. Then, in an instant, Buehl scaled the ladder, bounded onto the upper deck to the chorused shrieks of the ship's patrons and vanished within the restaurant.

Tam and David rushed over to Asher. 'You're hurt!' Tam said.

'Just a flesh wound.'

The walkie-talkie in Dodd's hand crackled with a static rush of words. 'He just left the restaurant and pushed his way out through the patrons. Nobody injured.'

'Come on,' Asher said. 'I want that bastard.' They raced through the restaurant toward the lower deck. Tam and David followed quickly behind. Two uniformed police officers stood near the entrance, Asher and Dodd talking hurriedly to them. Claire and Annie Belle stood beside them, their relief visible as David and Tam headed toward them unharmed.

'Tam, you and David stay on this ship with the girls,' Asher told her. 'Over there with the officers.'

She watched Asher and Dodd rush off ship, their walkie-talkies crackling. 'Are Murphy and Tony still in the parking lot?' Tam asked, hugging David, grateful they were safe.

'As far as I know. Probably sitting in some police car,' Annie Belle assured her.

Tam pursed her lips and held David tighter. He didn't resist.

'At least they're safe,' she said.

'Asher was hurt?' Claire's hand shook slightly. Love and truth were not aboard the *Moshulu* today.

Tam reached over and stilled her hand. 'He said it was a flesh wound.'

David leaned his head against his mother's shoulders. 'Mom, I'm never going to argue with you again.'

She wrapped her arms protectively around him. 'Don't get soppy on me,' she said, hugging him again, 'or make promises you can't keep.'

★　★　★

Buehl raced through Penn's Landing with Asher, Dodd and Colby in pursuit. But someone else was in pursuit of Walter Buehl. Someone who had to tell his brother not to hate him anymore, that he was sorry for what had happened countless years ago and that it would never happen again.

Tony Buehl had sneaked away from his police guard, slipping into the crowd, deliberately disobeying orders. To find Walter. To tell him he was sorry. To be forgiven.

★   ★   ★

Walter Buehl had run out of time and space. He had run to the end of Penn's Landing, jumped the chain blocking off the small private pier, and backed himself into a watery corner. He stood at pier's end, the waters of the Delaware behind him; Colby, Asher and Dodd in front of him, guns raised.

Buehl stared frantically at the few boats docked along the tiny pier. But the few residents on board had locked themselves securely inside.

No way out.

'Drop the gun, Buehl,' Asher shouted.

Asher, Colby and Dodd moved into modified combat stances five yards away from him. But Buehl still held the gun, his attention strongly focused on something to their left. Asher watched with stunned disbelief as Tony Buehl walked quietly past them and stopped within two yards of Walter Buehl.

'I come to talk to you, Walter,' Tony said simply.

Walter Buehl stared at Tony, struggling as confusion struck him again; seeing his brother, not in some distant past — no quarrelsome, threatening teenager — but a tiny man in his early fifties, looking at him with sad, beseeching eyes. 'You killed Mom!' he screamed viciously.

Tony shrank back a little to the left, then straightened up. 'I didn't mean it, Walt,' he said in a voice filled with mourning and a need to bury their past.

Thank God, Asher thought, *he's out of our line of fire*. But Walter Buehl's gun was now aimed at Tony, who was uncomfortably close to his brother.

'You're no good!' Buehl shrieked.

'No! I done wrong, but I paid for it. I didn't mean to hurt Mama, but I was holding that stupid knife from helping her with dinner and we were angry, so angry, and we fought. And we knocked a stupid bowl of eggs on the floor while we were fighting, and we slipped, both of us, and I was holding the knife, and she fell straight into the knife!' Tears cascaded down his face. 'And I paid for it every day of my life since I done that, Walter. And I never told no one it was an accident because I felt so guilty, and no one woulda believed me anyway! I just wanted to die, to lie down and hide myself from people for ever and ever. But it was an accident! *I never meant to hurt Mama!*'

His brother Walter glared back at him with a twisted, maniacal horror. 'No,' he raged in a low rumbling tone. 'You killed Mama, and it wasn't no accident. You're no good! You're no good!'

Asher watched Tony take a step closer to his brother, arms out in supplication. He raised his voice as loudly and as firmly as possible without shouting. 'Tony . . . stay where you are. Don't go any closer.' He saw Walter Buehl raise his gun again, pointed at his brother. 'Don't, Buehl!' he warned.

Tony turned helplessly toward Asher. 'I

got to make him understand!' He turned back to Walter. 'Please!'

'*No good!*' Buehl screamed. '*And you're gonna pay!*'

'*Don't, Buehl! Give yourself up!*'

Two shots were fired simultaneously. Walter Buehl's arm lurched backward as Asher's bullet snagged him in the shoulder. The bullet Walter had marked for Tony sank into the Delaware River. He sank to the wooden slats of the pier as if his shoulder wound was fatal. John Dodd walked over to him, his revolver pointed at the collapsed man lying on the pier. Walter's eyes were glazed, still fixed on Tony. Dodd cautiously removed the gun with the silencer from his limp hand.

Tony walked hesitantly over. 'Is he going to die?' he asked Dodd.

'No,' Dodd reassured him, wondering at the little man's calmness.

Tony looked down at the prostrate figure of his younger brother. 'I didn't *mean* to *do it*, Walt,' he said, his voice a strange mixture, both forlorn and firm.

Walter Buehl gazed furiously up at him. 'Don't tell me that! You're no good.

You're no good.' The fury ebbed and his face took on a mask of grief. 'Don't tell me that after all these years! You're lying!' The rescue squad pulled up as he turned his face away from Tony. 'You're no good,' he mumbled and shut his eyes.

'I think he passed out,' Dodd said, as the attendants ran up with a litter. They lifted Walter Buehl onto it.

'Sergeant Colby will be going with you,' Asher told them. Turning to Colby, he said, 'Make sure you read him his rights as soon as he's awake. Then see he gets treated and returned to Homicide.'

'What about your arm?' Colby asked.

'It's just a scratch. I'll treat it myself at Headquarters. We'll meet you there. Get going.'

'Yes, sir.'

The attendants removed Walter Buehl to the rescue unit. Colby climbed in after them. The doors of the unit closed and they drove off.

Dodd looked over to Tony Buehl, still standing silently, staring across the Delaware to the Camden side. Grappling with thoughts they could only guess at.

'Pleased to do business with you anytime, Lieutenant Lowenstein,' Dodd said. 'I like the way you handled that.'

Asher smiled tiredly. 'The respect's mutual, Lieutenant Dodd.'

Dodd inclined his head toward Tony Buehl. 'I wonder what he's feeling right now.'

'I don't know. Over forty years, burying a fact like that.' Asher's voice trailed off. He walked slowly over to Tony and stood in front of him. 'Ready to go?'

'Yes. Can I go home?'

'Well, we'll go get Murphy and David and the girls. Then we have to go down to Headquarters for a little bit. We have to file a report.'

Tony nodded glumly.

'You know, you were pretty brave back there,' Asher said. They moved back up the pier.

'Was I, Lieutenant? It didn't do me any good. Walter didn't believe me. I been hurt all these years, thinking he wouldn't believe me.'

'You've been hurt enough,' Dodd said, walking alongside. 'Forget it for now.

Maybe someday he'll believe you. You should've told somebody years ago.'

'They wouldn't have believed me.' Tony's smile was quiet, accepting.

'We believe you,' Dodd said quietly. He lit a cigarette as they headed back to the *Moshulu*, dragging deeply on it.

'That's two more than I ever had before.'

'You'll have more, Tony,' Asher said.

★   ★   ★

Nine p.m., and all was well.

Walter Buehl had been treated and released from Thomas Jefferson University Hospital. Homicide had processed him, arresting him on the charge of three counts of aggravated assault: one for Pete Delaney, one for David Westington, and one for Tony Buehl. It would be up to the District Attorney's office to approve the charges of murder in the cases of Nicky Gambetti and Paul Mandel. For Walter insisted he had no memory of illegal involvement prior to Joseph Moscowitz's confrontation with him at the screen door, no memory at all between hearing the argument between Mary and Peter Delaney and Joseph Moscowitz's switching on the porch light. He also claimed memory loss in his confrontation with Tam and David aboard the *Moshulu*. Asher only hoped the lab would provide convincing data linking him to the deaths of Nicky Gambetti and Paul Mandel. Whether Buehl regained his moments of lost memory or not, Asher knew the man would plead insanity. He now sat in a holding tank at Headquarters, awaiting arraignment before the Bail Commissioner.

Dr. Robbins had been filled in on Tony's strange confession. He would start the necessary paperwork on Monday to let Tony stay with his new friends on Coulter Street as a foster home. Later on, Tony would go before the State Review Board, hopefully to win his release from years of incarceration. He now had many people willing to testify for him.

They all held up their coffee cups to him now in Homicide.

'To you, Tony,' Asher toasted him

proudly. 'To your patience and to your courage. And to your human dignity.'

As cups lifted to lips, Tony said, 'I don't know about the dignity, Lieutenant, but can I make another toast?'

'Sure, Tony. What do you want to say?'

Tony lifted his cup, watching his friends lift theirs in readiness to drink to his toast. Asher, Tam, David. John Dodd, Dennis Colby, Captain Anunzio. Dr. Robbins, a look of pride and wonder on his face. His new family: Santa Ana, Claire, Annie Belle, Murphy and Scrugs. And assorted police personnel glad to be in on this moment.

Tony raised his cup to his toast, to toast the miracle. 'To freedom,' he said happily. 'The best thing in the whole world. May we never forget that. Ever!'

They saluted his toast and drank.

THE END